Rock City

A NOVEL

G. D. Bowlin

Broken River Books

This is a work of fiction. All names, characters, places, and incidents ware the product of the author's imagination. Where the names of actual celebrities or corporate entities appear, they are used for fictional puposes and do not constitute assertions of fact. Any resemblance to real events or persons, living or dead, is coincidental.

ISBN: 978-1-940885-58-2

For Mom and Dad.

And Peter, I guess.

The following is a work of fiction.
If you think you see someone you know, you don't.
If you think you're in this, you aren't.

But I was probably thinking about you.

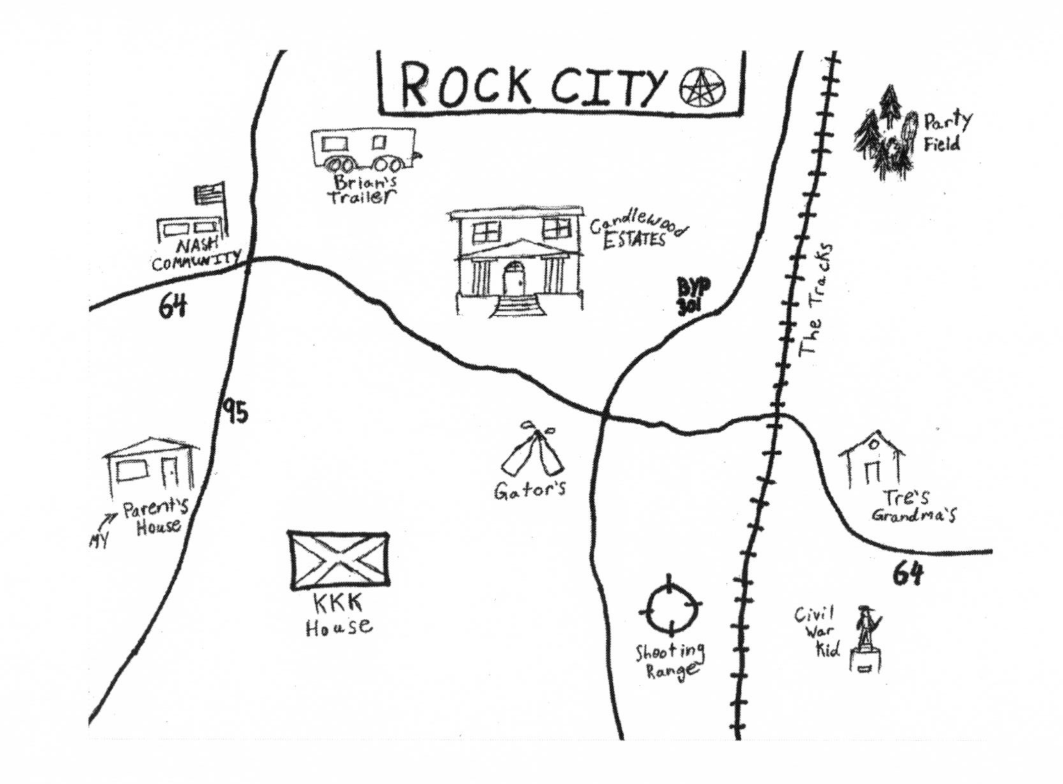
ROCK CITY
Brian's Trailer
Candlewood ESTATES
Party Field
NASH COMMUNITY
64
BYP 301
The Tracks
95
MY Parent's House
Gator's
Tre's Grandma's
64
KKK House
Shooting Range
Civil War Kid

Rocky Mount, NC
2005

SAFE

ROCKY MOUNT HAD A lot of names. A City on the Rise from their failed mid 90's tourism campaign. Murder Mount because of the violent crime statistics. Rock City because it almost made us feel like it was cool to be from somewhere no one had ever heard of.

No matter what you called it, it was a shithole and there was nothing to do.

The night that Newton Avery showed up I had been out of high school for a month and was spending a warm summer night getting a decent buzz going in a Waffle House parking lot. I think it was Thursday.

Tre and I were sitting on the trunk of his LeBaron with a stack of burned CDs in between us. The same CD running on a Discman duct-taped to the dashboard. Keys and bass and kick drum blasted spastic out of the car.

"This is my new band, Ambulance Arson," Tre said.

"Who, uh... who plays on this? Like, bass," I said.

"Oh, it's just me. I'm trying to do like a Jandek thing. A bunch of stuff that comes totally out of nowhere. I've been feeling super inspired lately, I've just been pumping songs out. I have another album's worth of stuff. I'm gonna put it out next month, probably."

My oldest friend, Tre. The first kid I met when my dad dipped out of the Army and moved us there. I was eight. People don't like new people around Rock City. Tre was okay with it and even then he was a weird kid. I liked him right away.

We used to play together but Tre always wanted to start with cover songs of other bands, agonizing until we unspooled the keys and chords and notes and nuances behind The Birthday Party or The Patti Smith Group or just fucking Joy Division. Tre said it was the only way to learn. I only wanted to play original stuff and I complained all the time. I didn't want to learn. After a while Tre quit calling me to rehearse. I pretended I didn't care.

"The guy from Superdrag found Jesus. Did you hear about that?"

"What's your fuckin' problem?" he asked.

"I'm good."

"No, you're doing that thing where you try to make cool stuff suck."

I shrugged. "Superdrag's not even that cool."

He snickered at me. He pulled a Pall Mall from under the brim of his camo trucker hat. It said "White Tail Hunter" on it with a woman's ass in white panties. Rednecks constantly tried to kick the shit out of him for it. He lit up.

"Do you want hashbrowns? I kinda want hashbrowns," I said.

"Smothered, covered, and capped."

"Smothered, diced, fingered, and thrown in a river."

"That's fucked," Tre said. We laughed until something caught his eye across the street. "Fuck."

"What?" I followed his look to a gas station where a Black dude came out carrying a forty and a bunch of Nerd rope. "You know that guy?"

"He's looking for my cousin," Tre said. "Which means he's looking for me."

"Okay, but why's he looking for *you*?"

He rolled his eyes. He knew what I was really saying was "*You're mixed, and you listen to The Unicorns so what the fuck?*"

He ran his hands through his loose curls and pulled his flannel shirt tighter around him. Tre dressed like Kurt Cobain. He didn't go in for girl jeans and extra small Blood Brothers t-shirts like me. He wore the flannel even when it was 90 degrees, and the humidity was like wading into a pool. I asked him why once and he told me it was his armor, and I didn't ask anything else.

He watched the car until it drove out of the parking lot and disappeared down the road, hidden by the darkness allowed by broken streetlights.

High beams hit us in the face, and I winced. A brand-new Honda pulled into the parking spot next to us, overshooting the line by like a foot. Two girls climbed out, Bambi-legging it from being a little drunk. Kelly was a girl I went to school with. She was Indian. Like her parents were from India. She was from Tarboro. Only non-White chick in the scene. People talked about her like it gave us cred and it was weird.

The other girl was Grace. I'd hung out with her a few times at shows and stuff, usually with Kelly. She went to Senior High, so she was from a different world. Exotic. I was surprised she was still hanging around here after high school. People said she was smart, and I believed them. But I didn't know her well yet and most people were dumb, besides.

As they walked over Kelly said, "Check this out!" and raised her shirt and bra up in one go. Silver bars studded her nipples. They glinted in the fluorescent light of the Waffle House sign. Tonight would be a good night. She let us take a look. "Just got 'em today."

Tre pretended to cover his eyes, but he was obviously looking through his spread fingers. He said, "You're fucking crazy. It's awesome."

"Thank you." She tried to pull her shirt back down, but the bra got waylaid. "Ow, fuck! The underwire is like, caught on the bar..."

"What's an underwire?" I asked.

She struggled to get back in harness and stared at me like I was an idiot.

I said, "Your dad get you a new car?"

She gave me a weird, scrunch-faced look and rolled her eyes and said, "Shut up Allan, it's not *new* new."

It's cool to pretend to be poor.

Grace reached into a giant purse and started to root around.

I snuck a peek into the open bag. There was candy and gum and shit and a CD that still had the plastic frame on it from where she stole it at Best Buy. There was a little brown bottle of hydrogen peroxide in there too. She pulled a small, off-brand coffee can out of the bag. Set it on the hood of the car with a heavy thud. Change called out from inside.

"We almost have enough," she said.

Tre and I looked at her, dimly.

"For the tattoo," she clarified.

Drunk one night in a different parking lot, I'd promised a few of them that if someone could raise the $250 I would get a tattoo of a wizard on my ass holding a double-ended dildo that shot lightning with the words 'Ye Olde Pussy Wizard' under it. I'd forgotten about it until now.

"Oh, shit. What? Really?" Eyes wide. Trying to contain the worry of following through on drunken me.

Tre punched me in the arm. I pushed him away.

Kelly straightened her shirt. "Hell yeah, pussy wizard. It's happening."

"We're just gonna spend that money on beer, right?" Tre asked, giving me an out.

"And Bojangles," I said. "Four-piece tenders box."

This deal was coming up pretty good for me.

"Well, I guess you're a pussy at least." Kelly snatched the can off of the hood and Grace laughed.

Another car rolled into the parking lot. A purple PT Cruiser with 'wood' paneling.

I said, "I didn't know the douchebag parade was today."

No one laughed except Tre.

The girls watched it pull in, getting all wide-eyed and jittery. Started instinctively running their fingers through their hair, getting their side-swept bangs beautiful and swept. Grace put on lip gloss and handed it to Kelly without asking.

The car sped up and screeched to a halt diagonally across a nearby spot. A guy popped out of the car. Super skinny, dyed blonde, dirty white slip-ons, bandana around the neck. He cocked his head and did his best smirking impression of Sha-nae-nae or whatever the fuck.

"Hey, hey, hey!"

Kelly ran up to him and hugged him.

"Who the fuck?" I asked no one. Grace and Tre had followed her. I followed them.

Kelly turned to face us, her arm around this smiling, charming, would-be Sha-nae-nae.

"This is Newton," she said. "He's from Chapel Hill."

At Chapel Hill, even Tre nodded in approval.

She said, "We met him on Myspace."

I fucking hated Myspace. Ranking friends and sharing every thought. Listing the most obscure bands. Making up fake ones to trick people. I did use it to crank down on people I knew who posted hot shit on there. Still, I wasn't proud of that.

"Call me New," he said. "Hey Grace, can I see your hands?"

Gripping her sleeves in place with her pinkies so that her wrists and palms were covered, she held them up like weird little paws.

"Perfect," he said.

In the back of the PT Cruiser there was a safe. The bottom right corner of the back of it had been pried open.

"I stole it from work. They fired me first so, you know, fair's fair. I got part of it off, but I couldn't get in there. I need your little hands, Grace. There should be at least five grand in there. This is going to be an exquisite evening."

I didn't like that he had an opinion on Grace's hands, but there was a passport for a woman named Velda, naked Polaroids of a different woman who looked a little young, and two thousand three hundred and thirty-one dollars in there and we took New down to Gator's where they serve people our age and he paid for everything all night.

PISS

I WOKE UP WITH a hangover. My first bad one. This was a few days later, after Tre and I had spent the night before drinking Old Es and Rebel Yell and fighting over whether straight edge kids could actually be punk and then what the word punk actually meant. I couldn't remember which side I was on.

My jeans were in a pile by the bed, soaked through with piss. They'd seemed like a convincing toilet the night before. It had dripped down into the hardwood. I got yelled at when I didn't use a coaster on the table.

"Fuck," I said.

It must have been the water I'd been slamming before bed. Mom said it was a hangover cure.

Kicked the jeans under the bed. Cracked the window and lit a cigarette, held my mouth to the screen. The heavy, humid air soaked through the mesh and into me. Smelled like rain coming on.

Through the screen I saw Delta, the woman next door. Stooped over in her husband's old clothes. Pleated khakis pulled tight to her withered waist with a length of rope. Her limbs were frail and stick-like, moving apprehensively, feeling for vibrations in the air. Like a praying mantis.

She tossed kibble out to the stray cats that lived in the yard behind her house. They rioted around her, mewing and hissing and shoving and biting at each other. She waved a claw at me.

"Hello, Greg!" she said. My dad's name.

I waved back. I took a final drag and stuffed the spent butt into a soda bottle I had sitting on the nightstand. I hosed the room down with off-brand Febreze. It covered the smoke pretty good. The piss, not so much.

I tiptoed out of my bedroom. Silence. The house was empty. I checked the time on the microwave. A little after noon. If I started walking now I could make it to and from the Shell Station that didn't card before my mom got home from teaching third graders.

The grass along the state highway was nearly knee high and all I could find was a pair of cargo shorts from middle school. I'd have to pick the ticks off my legs when I got back.

I still didn't know what I was going to do with the day. I got a little itch in the back of my brain, right back there where the wiggling stem injects itself into my spine. *Do something. Do anything*, the itch whispered.

Do something.

Whatever.

When I got to the Shell, the look the cashier gave me told me she didn't buy my shit and wasn't sure if selling tallboys to a kid was the right thing to do. It felt nice to be a moral challenge. I handed her a five and said keep the change and her doubt disappeared.

I threw the receipt into the trash can outside, dug out a rumpled but kinda clean Food Lion bag. Tucked the two cans inside. Now I was moving in secret.

The Taco Bell across the parking lot was looking pretty sexy. My hangover guts gnawed and groaned.

The girl behind the counter was pretty and stoned. She slid the tray to me. It was full. Cheesy Gordita Crunch. Little potato cup. Crunchwrap Supreme. I felt no shame under her red-rimmed gaze. I smiled.

"We gotta stop meeting like this," I said.

"Wha?" she said.

She gave me an annoyed look until I sat down, slouched in a corner, sucking hard on my Baja Blast.

"Allan."

I looked up. Newton was sitting on the other side of my table with some guy I'd never seen before. Earnhardt hat, ripped jeans. Disturbed shirt. Hiding behind Oakleys.

"We saw you through the glass," New said. "We're not eating here."

I hadn't seen him since he'd gotten us all wasted, and I wasn't sure what to do. The vibe was strange. I felt uncomfortable all of a sudden. Insecure.

The image of him buying us another round of Jaegers flashed in my head. His big grin, handing me the shot. Him reffing me and Tre shotgunning beers against each other in the parking lot even though he wouldn't do it himself. *Drink, drink, drink!*

He reached out and took my hand, gave it a few good, masculine shakes. His hand was callused, and I was surprised.

Oakley Hider watched.

I felt like I had to say something. I didn't.

New nodded at the Oakley kid next to him. "This is Brian. He's my friend."

"What up, man? We met the other night at that bar with y'all. This dude bums mad smokes." He jerked his thumb at New, clarifying.

The kid, he had one of those faces, those faces where most things are too small except for his lips and the center of it is all pinched up like an asshole, but the outside is all kind of slack so that you just want to hit him even though you'll feel bad right after.

"Good to meet you," I said.

He perked up. Like he hadn't heard that enough in his life. "You too." To New, "I gotta use the lavatory."

The words hung there for a second until New said, "Oh. Yeah." and the guy got up and left.

When he was out of earshot, I asked, "Lavatory?"

New leaned into me and whispered, loudly. "You look bad. Like the end of *Philadelphia* bad. You look ill, Allan."

"I was drinking last night. Again."

"Headache?"

I nodded. He fidgeted for a second, then looked around. Nobody was watching. Under the table, he pressed something into my palm. A pill, small and white. It was already sweating out in my hand.

He whispered, quietly. “It’s a Perc. Au revoir headache.”

I popped it in my mouth. Blasted it down, Baja style.

“Where’d you get this?” I asked.

“They’re Brian’s. I shouldn’t be giving them away but it’s okay. He likes you.”

“How do you know?”

“He likes everyone. In fact...” He thought about it for a second. “We’re going to Gator's. You want to come? Tomorrow night.”

“Um, yeah, I guess. I mean, I don’t have anything to do.”

JOB

THEY STARED AT ME from across the kitchen table. The light hanging overhead made it all feel like an interrogation. It kind of was. I'd broken the agreement. The code. I had to be dealt with.

I shifted uncomfortably in the chair, and it creaked in reply. One leg was shorter than the others and I moved again, tapping the leg onto the linoleum floor. And again.

"Your chair is like, messed up. It's uneven."

My mother rolled her eyes. My dad sighed, rubbed his temples. The honor of the family was at stake. His name, continuing on into the world. Already it was not what they had anticipated it would be.

"You had so much potential," my mom said.

"*Has*. Has so much potential," Dad corrected.

"Yeah, okay. Sure." The familiar sarcastic edge to her voice.

"I've only been out of school for... I don't know, like a month."

"You've been living in this house for a lot longer than that," she said.

She got up and went to the fridge, pulled out a half empty bottle of Riesling. She poured a healthy amount into an old Florida State Champions cup that my dad wouldn't get rid of and stood at the counter. Total power move.

"Can I have one?" I asked.

Dad stiffened even more. He could have had his spine surgically removed and his Army training would still hold him upright, in perfect posture, defying God and man and skeletal structures everywhere.

"You know, you could always enlist," he said.

"I was thinking about that." And I wasn't totally lying. My SAT scores had been decent, and the phone calls were numerous. They'd offered me a lot. But when I thought about wearing a uniform and getting yelled at to climb a wall my guts started to burn white hot. "I don't want to shoot anything, but I thought I could be a journalist. A guy said I could write for the Marine Corps Times."

Dad arched an eyebrow. "The Marines?"

"That's not him Greg, he doesn't have the discipline for that."

"Don't sell him short."

"I'm not, it's just true. I'm not being unfair." She turned on me. "Allan, am I being unfair? Do you have the discipline for the Marines?"

"I- I don't know. Maybe. No. Not yet. Don't they *make* you have the discipline? Like, while paying you?"

Mom took three quick drinks from the plastic cup. The Seminole mascot nodded in approval with each tip. She didn't.

"What about the Air Force?" Dad suggested. "If you just enlist with them you don't even have to fly. You can just mow lawns and file paperwork. It's pretty, um... chill." Mom shot him a look. "Relaxed. Relaxed environment, over there. Could be good to help you get your footing."

"He just needs to get a fucking job," she said to him. "You just need to get a fucking job," she said to me. I shifted in the chair and felt it smack against the plastic floor. She went back to Dad. "He won't listen to me. Tell him what we talked about. About what needs to happen if he's going to stay here." Then, back to me again. "I love you so much, but you're a goddamn adult now and you won't listen to me." She drained the cup.

"Your mom and I have been talking," Dad said. "You can stay here if you want to. Or need to. We're not going to kick you out. Yet. But there are conditions. You can't just lay around here and go hang out at the Huddle House with Travis."

"Tre, that's his friend," Mom corrected.

"Yeah, that kid."

I wished that I could tell them the truth. I didn't actually want to leave at all. I wanted them to help me. I was scared.

Instead, I said, "Okay. What do I need to do?"

"You can stay here for the next six months. Up to." He looked at my mom, then down at the table. "Things are a little tight. We can't feed you forever. After six months you have to figure out what you're doing. Until then you have to do two things: One, you have to go to Nash Community and sign up for a couple classes. Get some college credits. We'll pay for them. Just two of them."

I hated school. "You can't feed me, but you can pay for college classes?"

"Maybe you should say thank you because you're very lucky and not question it," Mom said.

"Sorry," I said.

Dad continued. "And you have to go to therapy. We both think that you might need a little help right now. My insurance will cover it."

I stood up, almost knocking the chair onto the ground. "*I* have to go to therapy?" I pointed at my mom, "She's the one who should-"

"Don't be a shit," she said.

"Sit down. Now," Dad said.

I did. Mom poured another splash of Riesling and glared at me. Then she said, "We're not indicting you or anything. You're not fucked up, but you need someone to talk to. This isn't a negotiation."

"Your mom is right. This one is final."

I didn't understand how they knew. How they could have seen something weird in me. Something I had been afraid to see myself. I knew they were right. But I didn't want to admit it. 'Cause fuck them 'cause they're parents.

But they had a house, and I had no idea where to go.

"Okay. I'll go."

"What do you say?" Mom asked.

"Thank you."

SUIT

My name was Walton St. Stevens. It was the name that came into my head when I saw the suit in the Goodwill. New said that we had to name whoever we were going to become in the new outfits. So, Walton St. Stevens was born.

It was a gray three piece made out of some kind of blend of wool and polyester or something and it was hot as fuck, and I couldn't stop sweating.

So fucking hot. The Mike's Hard Lemonade in my hand was rapidly warming into piss. Cicadas screeched from the tree line surrounding the field we'd pulled into off the dirt road. They made it feel like the whole world was vibrating around us. It was exciting and alive.

Percocet helped. We'd all blown a couple rails off the dash. It made the sun shine brighter. The green fields were emerald infinity. The pills made the nothing feel like something.

Like everything.

New had been driving a van this time, one of those maroon Caravans from the mid 90's. There was a picture of a clean-cut

Christian family taped on the dashboard. When I pointed it out, he'd ripped it off and tossed it out the window.

He came strutting around the van, zipping up a pair of flared out 70's jeans, topped with an R. Kelly t-shirt. The shirt said "Bump n Grind Rap" on it. New was scratching at his junk so hard I thought his nails were gonna pop off like that girl in the well in *Silence of the Lambs*.

"These bell-bottoms make my penis tip itch," he said.

"Welcome to crabs, dude. The guy that wore those last probably didn't wear underwear either."

"Fuck underwear. My hog can't be constrained."

He tossed me a pack of Kamel Reds. They were expensive, almost $3.50. I gave him a look and he said, "I got 'em from the dollar bin. They're expired."

I lit one. "What's the point of this? Like, dressing up and shit?"

"You can transform. You can be whoever you want to be. That's existentialism 101. That's the point of being alive. You don't have to have a shitty name like Allan anymore or have such a shitty attitude. For example, half an hour ago, I was Newton Avery. Now my name is Tyrese Wong. Who knows what the fuck Tyrese Wong is gonna do."

"I... I don't get your character."

"I do what I feel."

I downed the rest of my warm, steamy lemonade, and hucked it through the air. It landed in the cotton field twenty feet away. Reading my mind, New tossed me another and I cracked it open. From the van I heard the girls fumbling with the handle and swearing.

New sidled up close and said real low, "Can't wait to see Kelly in that outfit. She's so hot and, what do you think, like 4'11? I wanna grab her tiny ass by the ankles and hold her upside down like a big drippy trash bag and eat her pussy out."

"...Jesus," I said.

The back of the van opened. Pot smoke poured out and Kelly and Grace stumbled outside, giggling. I waved the skunk smoke away. Weed didn't do anything but make me paranoid.

Kelly had on Dickies coveralls that she'd cut the sleeves and legs off. They rode so high I could see the brown crescents of her ass cheeks sneaking out beneath. Grace was a little more conservative. She wore a tutu she'd found in the kid's section and a men's business shirt she'd knotted up to show off her stomach a little bit.

Kelly held her digital camera in the air and the girls crouched down and smiled up at it. Click. Bigger smile. Click. Sexy one, finger in mouth. Click. Goofy one, tongues out, mouths wide, still kinda sexy actually. Click. More, more, more.

Then they were done.

"We're hot," Kelly said. "These are gonna look sick. I'll post them tonight and call you."

"Wait, stop," New commanded and they stopped. "What are your names?"

"I'm GG Manson." Kelly turned the camera back on herself and gave the middle finger to the flash.

"I'm Sylvia Piaf," Grace said.

She took the camera from Kelly and aimed it at me. I looked down the barrel, frowning.

"Oh, come on, you look good in a suit. Don't be an asshole."

"Fine." I stabbed the smoke between my lips and posed in a way I thought would make me look cool.

"Those are good, those are good," Grace repeated. She tossed the camera to me.

"Hey, my mom bought me that, be fucking careful!" Kelly punched her in the arm.

I caught the camera, barely, one handed. Delicately, I set the alcohol down, digging it into a little bed in the warm, soft earth.

Through the lens of the camera, Grace looked tight-featured, strong, almost severe, in a way that I liked. She brushed her dark bangs out of the way. The thick black makeup around her eyes made them pop like an old silent movie star. She looked at me, not into the camera. She didn't do anything sexy or goofy. She didn't even smile like people do for pictures. She just gave a little grin all to me.

She was suddenly surrounded by a thick haze. New had lit up a bowl. The smoke clung to her like clouds, like she was a giantess, walking the earth, head in the heavens.

"Be careful with the camera, fuck face!" I heard Kelly yell.

Click.

MOMENTS

THERE WERE THREE BOOKSTORES in Rocky Mount.

There was the Books-A-Million at the mall so kids could play Yu-Gi-Oh and moms could buy coffee.

There was Sunrise Books and School Supplies. They got by because they were the only place in town that sold classroom supplies to teachers. I'd worked there for about six months during my senior year but got fired when the owner caught me giving an employee discount to Tre and stocking the Bible in the fiction section because I was listening to a lot of Minor Threat and reading Abbie Hoffman, I guess.

And there was Reader's Corner, a tight little tinderbox adjoining a mechanic's garage. They had piles of dusty used paperbacks, mostly romances and mysteries solved by cats in tea shops. Helping Rocky Mount's nanas kill time. Near as I could tell they were the only store that actually sold any books. They also bought books, and it was there that I brought a cardboard box full of my high school reading list so that I could pay a homeless guy to buy me a case of beer.

I shoved the box across the worn wooden counter at the old woman. She peered at me over smudged eyeglasses. "You're selling?"

"Yep," I said.

"Cash or credit?" She leaned over the box to get a better look and the glasses fell off, landing on a dog-eared copy of *East of Eden*. "Oh, shoot."

"Cash."

"Saving up for college, hm?" she asked, not bothering to pick the glasses up.

"Something like that."

"Wonderful. Just wonderful. I need to sort. See what I can sell."

"Cool, I'm gonna walk around outside." I had half a pack of Bailey's Lights in my pocket to kill some time with.

Something stopped me. The top of a head, gliding behind a bookcase. Bright red hair freshly dyed. A black beret neatly clasped. A hand reached up to push a lock back. Short fingernails, spotty black nail polish chipped and picked at. I pursued, rounding the corner of the bookshelf to find Grace standing there, studying spines.

I liked seeing her away from everyone, in her own element. Copy of *The Bell Jar* held tight to her chest like a protective talisman, narrowed eyes reading every title on the shelf, saying them out loud in a tiny whisper meant only for her.

Something had happened inside me and I was already in love with her.

"Grace?" I said.

She turned. She wore a raincoat and miniskirt combo. Neither were right for the weather. "Oh," she said. She smiled.

"I thought that was you." I didn't know what to do with my hands. I waved. Weird.

She waved back. "What are you doing here?" More surprised than anything.

"Selling off some books from my AP reading list. Another copy of *Cold Mountain* is about to make it into circulation." I was proud of myself for including my status as a former AP student. Prouder, when she sorta laughed at the *Cold Mountain* joke.

"Sometimes you can find good stuff here between all the Harlequins and James Pattersons."

"I would've thought you'd already read that one."

"Huh?" She raised an eyebrow, then remembered *The Bell Jar*. "Oh. Yeah, I've read it a couple times. This is mine actually, from home, I'm reading it again. Have you?"

"No, not yet. I'm just trying to prepare myself. I just know it's gonna wreck my weekend, you know?"

"You can borrow mine," she said. "When I'm done with it."

"Excuse me, young man?"

The old woman was raised up on her stool on her knees, surprisingly agile, and was waving a book in the air like the victim of a hideous car crash with a flare. A Bible I'd been given at birth by some well-meaning relative. Its white cover had a big eyed, yellow-haired Precious Moments baby on the front. The book was pristine. Never been used.

"You accidentally put your bible in here." The old woman's glasses had gone crooked in the action, and she pushed them up her nose.

"No, I didn't."

"I... ah," she said, wrinkled mouth frowning, an overwhelming sadness in her voice.

"Ooh," Grace knocked me in the arm with her elbow. "You're edgy."

"You wanna go pick up some beer with me? The guy who doesn't card is working the Grab n' Go tonight."

BRACED

COMING INTO THE PARTY with Grace made me feel like I wasn't a piece of shit. She was smart and nice. When we walked in people who I didn't even know were saying hi to her and it felt like they were saying hi to me too.

A couple people almost knocked us over carrying this wasted girl we called Poopswing. One guy had Poopswing's ankles and the other had her wrists and she was hanging upside down like a pig on a spit. She was moaning, incoherent. Kelly was following them, and she turned to Grace's troubled look and said, "It's okay, they're putting her in the guest room. She's safe."

Then Grace got pulled into a group of girls with sideways stud belts and short hair with long bangs and feathered spikes in the back. Someone in the crowd was smoking a clove cigarette and the sickly-sweet smell covered everything.

I went to the kitchen where I found Tre hiding from the crowd. Someone had brought Wild Turkey 101 and we did a couple shots together and talked about his upcoming performance art project, Neo-Nihi-Cataclysm. He was going to dress in drag like Gwendolyn Brooks and get mock executed by cops while our buddy Dank wore a horse mask and played the saw against the soundtrack for the movie Bruce Almighty.

"Do people know immediately what Gwendolyn Brooks looks like?" I asked. "I don't think people are gonna get it, man."

He nodded sagely. "Then they definitely won't get Mel Lyman. I was gonna have somebody play Rock of Ages on the harmonica while getting blown by Charles Manson."

There was an energy in the air that night. Restless and animal. There was going to be a fight. Everyone could feel it. It was just a matter of who was gonna throw the first punch.

"How well do you know Grace?" Tre asked. I guess I looked defensive because he followed it with, "You guys came here together, so I'm just wondering. I've known her forever, we went to YMCA day camp together, so..."

"We bumped into each other at Reader's, it was like, totally random. Is this a dibs thing?"

"Dude, come on, I'm not a fucking bro dick. Also, I'm not into her. She's great, she's a good person. She's my friend. I'm just saying, you know, get to know her."

"Get to know her how? Is she a murderer or something? I don't think I'd have a problem with that."

New moonwalked into the kitchen. He was actually pretty good, somehow gliding over the sticky mess all over the linoleum floor. He came to a stop in between us and hopped up on the counter.

"Oh, hi," Tre said flatly.

"I move like a beautiful gazelle," New said.

"You're the White Gregory Hines. I tell everyone that." I cracked open a beer.

"I'm post-racial, thank you. Whose house is this?"

"Dank's," Tre said.

"He's back from the Navy? I don't even know why he signed up. His parents are rich," I said.

"Yeah, I don't know. Anyway, his parents went on a trip to visit his older sister, an ER doctor or something living in Baltimore for some reason. So yeah."

"Dank. Awesome." New pointed from the kitchen and out into the living room. "And who the fuck is that?"

We turned to find this fucking guy Jonathan eased way back like that deflated girl in the weed commercials. He was looking down the hallway where they'd just taken Poopswing. He was wearing skinny jeans and a vintage tuxedo shirt and a vest. A few feet away, Brian was watching him while sipping from a beer can at a steady, almost automatic pace, like one of those desk tchotchke birds that dips in and out of a glass of water.

"That's Jonathan..." Tre said, uneasy.

"Jonathan? Not Jon or Jonny? He actually makes people call him Jonathan? Why does he dress like a magician for pedophiles?"

"Oh, he's like a known pervert," I said. "He tried to pick up on what's-his-nuts' thirteen-year-old sister after a show one night."

"What's he doing here? You let people like that in your scene and they'll infect it. Like a felonious, cummy virus."

"He claimed he didn't know how old she was." Tre didn't sound convinced, but I knew him well enough to know that he just wanted everyone to get along. Give them enough time and no one ever did, though.

"Shit. I heard she was wasted, and someone caught him taking her to his car," I said.

Tre's brow furrowed. This was news. He turned to me. "Can you help me keep an eye on him please?"

I gave him a thumbs up.

Then he said, tipping his beer in Brian's direction, "Who's that?"

"That's Brian. He's cool," New said.

Tre ignored New, kept eyes on me.

I said, "He's cool."

New tapped the top of his bottle neck to mine. Kissing tips. He hopped off the counter and walked away. Tre watched him go.

"I gotta change the music, this faux aggressive sing-songy Cursive shit is irritating." He left too.

I was alone in the kitchen. It was a party.

Later I walked around, trying to find Grace while trying to look like I wasn't looking for her. I didn't find her. I didn't find Jonathan either. His space on the couch was empty. Brian was still standing near the hearth nursing the same beer, spacey. I grabbed him by the arm, and he looked at me, startled.

"Hey man, did you see where the guy with the vest went?"

"Nah, he's a squirrely lil fucker though. I had a fucked up feeling so I was kinda watching him and shit but then I started talking to this super hot brownish chick."

"That's Kelly."

"Oh shit, she didn't tell me. She's super hot."

"Yeah," I agreed.

I looked in the bathrooms, but they were all empty except for the one where I walked in on some girl I didn't know throwing up in Dank's parent's bathtub and she screamed at me. He wasn't in Dank's sister's perfectly preserved childhood bedroom where Dank was playing a Xiu Xiu cover to a few girls sitting around on the floor. He wasn't in the backyard either. Just a bunch of us smoking. My palms were sweating, and my stomach started to feel sick. We had a Jonathan problem. I looked around but I couldn't find Tre. Everyone fell into a black hole. Except Kelly. She was leaning against the railing of the deck, eating out of a can of Pringles. Her eyes were bloodshot weed red.

"Hey, can you take me to the room where Poopswing is passed out?"

"Who the fuck is Poopswing?"

"Riley, sorry. In 10th grade the girl's bathroom went out and she took a dump under a- Never mind. Riley."

"That's a super weird request, dude." She offered me a Pringle.

"I think something like, bad might be happening and I need you to come check on her with me." I took her by the elbow and walked her inside. She dropped the Pringles can on the floor and someone immediately walked over them, grinding them into the carpet.

She led me through the living room, down a hallway to the end. There was a door with a sign that said "Be Our Guest" on it in that curly southern lady font that they were always using to put their initials on their purses. Kelly went to knock, but I motioned for her not to. No warning was better. She pushed the door open.

Poopswing was laying in the bed, on top of the covers. Dead to the world. Jonathan stood beside her, at the edge of the bed. We couldn't see him from the front, but his pants sagged around his waist and his left arm was jerking furiously. The sound of the party boomed in once we opened the door and without turning around he knew someone was there and he started to button himself up. Kelly and I both froze for a second and he turned to face us before we advanced on him.

"Hey guys, I was just checking on-"

Kelly slapped him across the face, and I grabbed him around the back of the neck and started moving him toward the door. He hadn't actually buttoned the pants up apparently and they started falling down his legs.

"Wha- what's, uh?" Poopswing came to for a second and Kelly said something reassuring.

I shoved Jonathan out into the hallway. He slammed into the wall and slid backward onto his ass, newly flaccid dick hanging part way out of his boxers. Kelly stayed in the room and shut the door. He kept trying to talk but I didn't listen. I was on him in a second, blindly hitting him. Uncontrolled.

Like a pack of gazelles, house party kids know when there is trouble. The only difference is, they run toward it. We were surrounded by people in seconds. Everything was a blur, and I had no idea who was there or what they were saying.

I just kept hitting him.

He had tried to fight back at first, but I'd been on him quick. He was disoriented. Confused, I guess. After a few punches he just lay there, taking it. I didn't know he had braces until one of them cut my knuckle open and I didn't know that he was unconscious until Dank pulled me off of him.

I backed against the wall and looked at what I'd done. Blood was splattered on the carpet, smeared on the wall, covering Jonathan's face. Everyone was looking at me. Some worried, some confused, some scared. New gave me a thumbs up from the back of the crowd. Dank slapped Jonathan awake. He got him to his feet, but held him against the wall, not letting him go. Jonathan looked around, scared. A broken tooth hung in his bloodied mouth, suspended by his braces. I felt good about myself.

Kelly stepped out of the door behind me, shut it quietly. When she saw Jonathan she gasped and covered her mouth. Tre pushed his way through the gazelles and took everything in. He got it.

"Get the fuck out of here, man."

Tre led him through the already thinning group of watchers. The action was done. The blood was over. Now it was time for music and drugs and fingering.

Kelly and Dank and I were left in a circle in the hallway.

"She's okay," Kelly said, but she didn't sound like she was sure she meant it.

"Okay, good. Thanks guys." Dank assessed the bloody damage to his mother's plush carpeting. Looking at the carpet, it occurred to me that his parents made a lot more money than mine did.

"You really went apeshit on him, huh?" Dank asked me.

"Sorry, I... I didn't realize what I was doing. I... I couldn't stop." My hand was bleeding.

He patted me on the back. "It's okay. It's good. I'll try to... I dunno, clean it up if I can. You guys go back in there."

Stumbled into a bathroom. Ran my hands in the cool water. It was soothing and I hoped that my cut wouldn't get infected too bad. I wrapped my hand in a towel with flowers embroidered on it.

Kinda dazed. I wandered back into the party, through people yelling at each other to drink and arguing over music and integrity and making out and drinking. Some of them avoided my eyes.

My legs took me into the backyard where someone handed me a cigarette and lit it for me, and I took it, and someone offered me weed packed into the top of an apple, but I said no.

I sat down on the edge of the deck, as far away from people as I could. I inhaled deeply and then let it out. Watched the smoke rise, a ghost from the grave in the night. Somebody said, "You have some blood on your shirt."

I looked down at my blue t-shirt with a black line graphic of Mel Gibson from *Mad Max* on it. Blood covered Max's little dog. Dingo? Dog. I followed the voices. Grace sat a few feet away from me, almost hidden in shadow.

"Do you have another cigarette?" she asked. From my back pocket I pulled the crushed pack of Baileys. She scooted next to me, and I handed them over. She took one, lit it, kept the pack.

"Thanks," she said.

"What are you doing all the way out here?" I asked.

"Hiding like a ghoul in the shadows?"

I nodded and she gave a little laugh. "I have the hiccups. It's embarrassing."

"What's one thing that you love and one thing that you hate?"

She hiccupped. "What? Why?"

"My mom used to make me do this when I would get in a bad place. It's to get your mind thinking about other stuff. It works for hiccups too. You'll get distracted and forget to hiccup."

"Okay..."

"It works, I promise. What's one thing you love and one thing you hate?"

"I love... French onion soup. I hate... people who get animals high. They're just babies, they don't know anything." She looked out at some hidden place in the inky black backyard. A distant look in her eye. After a moment, she smiled. "No hiccups. It does work."

I held my palm up. She slapped it. She took a drag of her cigarette, and it was sexy.

She said to me, "Okay. What's something you love and what's something you hate?"

"Ah, man, I don't... I don't know. I don't have like, absolute feelings about stuff."

"What does that even mean? I did it, now you have to. It's fair. And it's right. I think you know that."

She was right. I did know that. "Fine," I said.

I tried to think of something that I loved. I liked books okay. I liked getting fucked up, but saying that's what you love isn't a good look. I loved music, that was the only thing I could think of, but it was so cliché I wanted to self-immolate right there in the backyard.

"Love is too hard. Can I do the hate one?"

She grinned, shrugged. *Sure.*

"I hate..." Even this should have been easier for me. I'd always felt like I hated everything but with her there I couldn't think of anything. I desperately wanted to hate the right thing. Instead, I said, "I hate people who say that they're into feet, like it's some weird, edgy fascinating fetish, when it's super common. It's like, 'Did you guys know I'm into boobs?' Shut up, you're not interesting. I think I'm kinda drunk."

She thought about this. "Is it really that common?"

Why the fuck had I started talking about feet? “Yeah, it’s pretty common.”

“Are you into feet?”

“Why, do you have high arches?” She blushed. I said, “I’m kidding. I’m not into feet. But if I were I’d be one of like, five billion people on the planet.”

“Dude, dude!” I heard New yelling at me from the house. “Come inside I have to tell you something super important. It’s an emergency!”

“Sorry. It’s an emergency, I guess,” I said. “I’ll see you inside?”

“You will,” she said.

New took me to a bathroom in Dank’s parent’s finished basement, which I didn’t even know he had, which was annoying ‘cause there was a foosball table in there and he knew I liked foosball. Brian was waiting in the bathroom, sitting on the top of the toilet tank. I liked that his cowboy boots were dug into the fancy plush, pink cover of the toilet seat lid. On the counter next to him there were three lines of blue powder and three beers.

“This is for you, my dude.” New closed and locked the door behind us.

“What, uh, what is this?” I asked.

“Morphine.” Brian said it like he was talking about a ham sandwich.

“Morphine? What the fuck, how did you get this?”

"I have tons of shit like this. I get migraines," Brian said. "So they prescribe me tons of these, all these different doctors, and I just sell the rest."

"I don't have any money..."

"It's fucking free, dumbass." New leaned over and sucked half of a line through his nose with a one-dollar bill.

"I share with folks I like," Brian drawled. "Like New, I like New. And you. I saw what you did to that fuckin' rapist. I like you."

"Thanks, dude."

New handed me the dollar bill. I leaned over and snorted a line of morphine. It made me feel the best I've ever felt in my entire life.

New slapped me on the back. "I really admire what you did to that guy. There was so much fuckin' blood man, just fuckin' sick as hell."

MATCH

"THE QUESTION FREQUENTLY ASKED around violent offenders is whether or not they can be rehabilitated."

Ms. Walton stared out at the classroom of twenty or so people. We ranged from what looked like sixteen to what was definitely fiftysomething. Everyone had a right to learn at Nash Community College. Behind her the words Criminology 101 were written on a white board. The school didn't offer a 102.

Tre shifted uncomfortably next to me. We'd decided to take the class together, thinking it would be fun. Fucked up stuff about serial killers. He pawed lightly at the bandage on his neck. He'd gotten new ink. So fresh I hadn't seen it yet.

"But what *I* believe should be asked is not whether they can be rehabilitated, but rather, do we believe that they're *worthy* of rehabilitation. Most Americans don't seem to think so. So, they don't even bother to try."

I'd seen her outside before class smoking thin cigarettes and stabbing them out when they burned to the halfway point. She was older with short, blonde hair. A tan pantsuit. 90's shoulder pads. Perfect French nails. I mean pristine. She looked like she could be mean to men who didn't meet her expectations. She was pretty hot.

"The violent crime rate in Rocky Mount is nearly triple that of the rest of the country. You live in the fourth most dangerous small city in the United States."

Tre spoke up. "Yeah? Where do you stay at?"

"I live in Raleigh. I commute in twice a week."

The group murmured and shook their heads. She kept on.

"One prime example of this concept of worthiness is the death penalty. It says that not only do we believe that violent criminals cannot redeem themselves, but also that they do not deserve the opportunity to try. After all, redemption could take a lifetime and we are taking that life from them." She waited for a moment, expecting a response. Nothing doing. She said, "What do you think about that idea?"

A middle-aged man in the front of the room spoke up. "That's not true. It takes a lifetime, ma'am. You can be redeemed or rehab'd or whatever in two seconds. Just talk to Jesus and accept him into your heart. You're forgiven for anything that way."

She nodded very deliberately and raised her eyebrows to indicate interest. "That's a unique point of view, thank you." Somebody give the nice mean lady an Oscar.

"The death penalty is totally messed up." Everyone turned to a girl sitting in the back of the class. It was the stoned chick from Taco Bell. Her bleached hair hung in hard, tight curls, looking like ramen noodles. She had her hand raised. "My daddy's on death row and it's bullcrap."

"Hm," Ms. Walton's eyes gleamed. Here was a young person who would make her point for her. "So, you think an injustice has been done here? Interesting. Can you tell us more?"

"He was just driving around with his friend one night and the friend wanted to mess this other guy up. So his friend, he went and found the guy and killed him. Daddy was just like, around, sort of, just driving the car."

"Interesting... Yes, there's a lot of debate around whether or not a driver should be charged as an accomplice if he didn't know that a murder was to take place."

"Yeah. Yeah!" the girl started to get excited. Stoney eyes came to life. She had someone in her corner, finally. "So when they found him, they got out of the car and-"

"Your father got out of the car?" Ms. Walton asked.

"Well, yeah, but still it's messed up, 'cause when they found the dude daddy just poured gasoline on him. His friend's the one lit the match."

"Oh. Huh. That is... tragic. I'm sorry to hear about your father." Ms. Walton casually walked back behind her desk, putting a defensive barrier between her and the rest of us.

The girl looked deflated. She lowered her hand.

Ms. Walton, in rapid fire, said, "Thank you for sharing a personal experience around this. This is an excellent segue into your next assignment. I'd like for you to put together a profile of someone on death row and present an argument both for and against their status. It can be someone 'famous' like a serial murderer." She put air quotes around famous. "Or someone you have a personal connection to like a um, relative. And that's as good a time as any to end class. I'll give you all ten minutes back today. Get your research subjects to me by next week." She took a breath.

Tre and I fell into step together on the way to the parking lot. The tattoo bandage rode up his neck, poking out from under his shirt. I wanted to ask but knew he'd reveal it when he wanted to. It needed to have healed up properly and look just right before it could be shown to the world.

"What are you gonna do your project on?" he asked.

"I dunno. Maybe that chick's dad. She's sorta cute."

"Fucking community college. You know, I'd be at a real school if I'd graduated from RM Academy." He spit through his teeth onto the pavement.

Our senior year Tre had gotten a scholarship to Rocky Mount Academy, an all-White prep school. They gave out two scholarships every year and he'd gotten one. The first Black kid to ever go. Two months later he was back in class with me at our normal high school where the toilet stalls had no doors and No Child Left Behind agents monitored our classes to try and improve literacy rates.

He said he'd gotten in a fight and been kicked out. He said he'd been jumped in gym class. That was all he told me, and I didn't ask. He'd doubled down hard on music after that and never mentioned the Academy again.

He detoured a few feet away to kick a rock. It pinged off a park bench, startling a kid who was sitting there reading. Tre snickered.

He said, "Nobody helped. I thought I had some friends there, too. The teacher finally stopped them, but I know he let it go on for at least a minute after he saw."

"Why'd they jump you?"

He looked at me like I had just asked him where sunlight came from. "I was the only Black kid," he said.

"I mean, you're Black-ish."

"If you have a drop of Black blood in you, you are Black. I am Black."

"I know. I make jokes when I get uncomfortable."

"I know."

"You don't think it was your love of Neutral Milk Hotel? Honestly, that probably got you more heat."

That made him smile.

We stopped next to his car, an Oldsmobile Delta 88. Cream white with maroon leather seats. Big as a yacht. His grandmother had given it to him when she gave up driving. He opened the door and threw his bag in.

"Love this Olds, man. Is this the part where you give me a Werther's and take me to K&W for a 4pm dinner?"

"Ay yo!"

The call cut through the engines and voices of the lot. A brand-new red Charger had pulled up behind us, blocking us in. The dude from the gas station was leaning out the window.

In a split-second Tre had the door open and he was reaching for something underneath the seat. Lightning went through me. Adrenaline. Breath caught in my throat. My heart stopped, but I didn't. I dropped my books and stepped forward, chest pumped out, hands tightened into fists.

The dude in the car held his hands out the window. Empty.

Tre froze. He didn't move his hand away from under the seat.

The dude smiled and flashed a gold grill. Said, "Yo dun, chill, chill." He laughed. "You got your White boy steppin' up, Tre. Where your cousin at?"

"I dunno, bro." Tre's voice was an octave lower than normal. "Ain't seen him in a minute."

"Yeah, aight." The dude ran his fingers against his chin. The math didn't seem to be adding up. "You sure? I know he your cuz but that nigga *sheisty*. You be doin' me a favor. I'd do you a favor then too, feel me?"

Tre didn't break eye contact with the guy. "Like I said, ain't seen him."

"Aight, cool. Nice lumberjack shirt, nigga. Lookin' like the muthafuckin' Brawny man." He laughed and his grill caught the sun. It was kinda beautiful. "Catch you on the flip, dun."

The car pulled out, but I couldn't relax. I bounced on the balls of my feet, flexing my fingers in and out. All amped up.

"Holy fuck. You were awesome. That was badass, Tre."

He shrugged and watched the car until it left the parking lot.

"What's uh... what's under the seat?"

His hand was still wedged under there. He pulled out something wrapped in an old towel. He opened it. A pistol, semi-auto.

He said, “It’s not a real Colt, but it is a 1911. Got it from Zion. Remember Zion from Charter School?”

“Yeah, I remember Zion.” He’d shown me his ass on the bus a lot. Without thinking I reached out to touch it. Stopped myself. “Sorry, can I hold it?”

“Yeah, just-” I raised it to get a closer look. “Don’t hold it up for people to see, dumbass. Jesus.”

It was surprisingly heavy. There was a scuff mark over where the serial number used to be. I set it down in the towel. He wrapped it up and tucked it back under the seat.

“My cousin pulled the trigger on a drive by a couple weeks ago. The cops will get him eventually. If that guy and his boys don't find him first. The gun, it’s a precaution really. Better to have it than not. Why are you smiling like that?”

He gave me a weird look.

He said, “I have to get the fuck out of this town.”

“You will. Wanna come over and put Moon Pies in the microwave?”

We bumped fists and climbed into the Olds.

All the way home I thought about that guy and his grill catching light and the idea that I could have been killed but hadn’t. The feeling it gave me. I liked it.

MOHAMMED

I'D NEVER DONE ADDERALL before, and I was so excited I wanted to snort it instead of waiting on my gut. New said cool but Brian reigned us in.

It was a sunny day and we wanted to feel up, so we went to a park across the street from the movie theater to take the speed. Brian showed us how to parachute by cracking open Adderall pills and letting the little spheres inside roll into scraps he tore off of some Wendy's napkins Grace had in her dashboard (*"I like, never eat there. Seriously."*) and we packed 'em up tight and swallowed them. Washed them down with a can of Monster energy from Brian's truck (*"Yeah I drink it, shit's good"*).

"Gonna hit y'all hard. Real soon. So get ready," Brian instructed.

It was me, New, Grace, Kelly, Brian, some guy whose name I didn't know, four Michelob Ultras and a giant bottle of Barefoot Chardonnay that Grace and Kelly had shoplifted from the Walmart in Grace's infinite purse.

We pulled a blanket from the car and laid it down in a clearing near an old statue of a Civil War soldier that looked like it hadn't been tended to in a long time. Without meaning to, we all instinctively sat down in a circle, cross legged like kindergarten kids, and waited to start having a good time.

New looked around the little clearing, at the decaying benches and the moss-covered statue.

"This looks like one of those parks where closeted gay dudes go to blow each other. Is this where you go to get your dick sucked by local dads, Brian?"

I laughed, but Brian didn't. He dug a small rock out of the dirt behind him and whipped it at New, who ducked out of the way. "Shut the fuck up, dude."

Grace wrinkled her nose. She'd sat close to me which I was glad for.

"Where's Tre?" she asked me.

I realized I hadn't talked to him in a few days, since the parking lot, which was a while for us, but I didn't want to say that. "I dunno exactly. He had something to do today."

Kelly said, "Probably practicing with Dank. Those guys are real. They play together all the time."

"Yeah," I shrugged. "I guess. Maybe."

New said something and the volume of his voice was jarring. The pill was taking hold.

My jaws started to feel tense, and my teeth felt dirty. I could feel my eyes for the first time in my life. My brain juice was flowing, hot and powerful.

Grace was getting it too. "People take this to feel normal?" she asked.

"Yeah, this is nuts. This shit is crazy. I feel like, happy," I said.

Brian laughed. "Yeah, it'll do that. You're about to focus on some piece of grass or shit for the next four hours."

"Or talking and talking and talking and talking," said the stranger.

I had to move around. I got up off the blanket and wandered over to the statue. I was a detective with a case. A puzzle to unravel. Who had died for this rock to be carved?

Weeds grew around the base, nearly a foot high. At the top stood a kid holding a rifle. Couldn't have been older than me. Looked even as young as fourteen. He was wearing one of those Civil War hats and had a blanket rolled up and wrapped around him. There was a plaque by his feet:

To all the young men who are no more. Thank you, the Daughters of the Confederacy.

"Ooooh shit," I said.

"What?" Grace asked.

"This statue of this little dude. It's a Daughters of the Confederacy thing."

Kelly rolled her eyes.

"I think my mom is in this. Or was," I said to no one in particular.

Brian was perched on a rock like a gargoyle, rubbing his arms which were naked in his sleeveless Slipknot shirt. "Mine was too. But you gotta pay those dues, boy. That shit is serious."

"It's so fucked up," Grace said.

Brian said, "This is North Carolina. We live in a place of rebels, dawg. I don't hate nobody, y'all know that. I'm cool with whatever. It's about like, embracing, standing up and saying fuck it. It's like punk."

"The Confederate flag is not punk," New said.

"You know what I mean."

"I don't think African Americans see it that way," Grace said.

We all looked at Kelly. She looked back. She said, "What? I'm fucking Indian, you dipshits." She turned to Brian. "But I don't think they'd agree with you. I don't anyway. Dawg."

Grace and I shared a secret grin. I didn't want to laugh at Brian. I liked him and he didn't know what he was talking about, like most people.

He shrugged. "That's cool. Anybody can feel whatever way about whatever. That's your rebellion. It's like a..."

"Paradox," New interjected.

"Yeah. Paradox. Anyway, I didn't mean to hurt your feelings."

"It's cool." Kelly said, though her face said it wasn't. She turned away from him and held the wine bottle up to the sun, like a paleontologist studying the first dinosaur bone. Perplexed and yearning. "We don't have a corkscrew, huh?"

Realizing the getting was good, Brian leapt off of the rock and landed on the balls of his feet like a cat. He moved stealthily away into the woods, picking up a big stick on his way into the thicket, disappearing into the forest completely after whacking the stick against the trunk of a tree and wincing at the vibrations running up his arm.

With Brian disappeared I needed to stare at someone else and work my jaw around. The stranger. He looked older than us. His face weathered. Mid to late thirties, I guessed. A scar ran across the top of his hand. Red and angry. He'd arrived with Brian and New and had barely spoken. Now he sat silently across from us, legs still pretzeled up under him. He watched us, but without creepily fixating on any one thing. A ghost taking in the world.

"Hey dude. What's your name?"

"Everyone calls me Mohammed, but-" he gestured to his White face. "That's not my name. People just call me that."

"Can I ask why?"

He shrugged. "Everyone does. I was in Iraq. Medic. I came back home, and everybody here thought it was funny to call me Mohammed. So. I dunno. You put up with what you can, I guess."

"Thank, uh..." Grace started to say then trailed off, as if she lost her place, then jolted a bit as she found it again. "Oh, uh-Thank you for your service."

"Yeah, yeah, thank you," Kelly added quickly.

"Sure. No problem."

"Medic, that's a, that's a big job. That's a lot," I said it like I knew something about it, and I regretted it immediately. "I hope you didn't see too much shit." I kept talking and didn't know why. I looked around for help, but the girls were locked up tight and New was gone too. Off with Brian, I guess. I wished

I'd gone with them. They were probably throwing rocks at shit and having fun together.

Thankfully, Mohammed took over and broke the silence.

"No more than anybody else. I mean, there's not a lot of dying out there. In Iraq at least. Compared to Afghanistan. That place is a shithole. I mean there's a lot of dying in comparison to, you know, going to Food Lion or something. Or Emerald Isle. You're more likely to get killed in Iraq than Emerald Isle. The big thing, you know, for medics especially, is the maimings and shit. Lots of hidden bombs on the roads and now they got this iron plating under the hummers, but that just knocks 'em around or straight up flips 'em up and even with plating you're gonna get shrapnel and even rocks and shit coming in. So, you know, it doesn't blow guys up, but they get all cut up, losing arms and hands and stuff. The worst though is getting knocked around. Your brain is like change in a piggy bank and it just gets ping, ping, ping, ping. All over. Nothing I can do about that. And I was good. So, you know, guys come home alive but... not okay. I did pick up some bodies outta rubble though if that's what you're asking."

We stared at him. Nobody said a word. We didn't know how to. He blinked, then. Seemed to realize where he was, then. Talking to kids who had no idea what death looked like.

"Sorry. Did I just say all that out loud? Sorry. I'm talking a lot."

"It's okay," Grace whispered. "I don't mean to be weird, but do you want to hold my hand?"

"That would be nice if that's okay," Mohammed said.

She scooted over next to him and put her hand down on the blanket. He reached out and took it, gently. They sat there together in silence.

"We don't have a corkscrew," Kelly said.

She got up and found two rocks, one wide and flat, the other small and sharp, almost like an arrowhead. Holding it at just the right angle against the big one, she was able to break off the neck of the bottle without shattering the rest of it. A little wine spilled out into the dirt.

"Eh, that was like, a nickel's worth of wine. This shit is cheap," Kelly said.

"Hey, that shit was free," Grace said.

Mohammed laughed. Kelly passed the bottle and we cut our mouths drinking and handing it around, becoming blood together in the park.

GOD

Rock City is actually made up of two counties: Nash and Edgecombe. Train tracks run along the county line, slashing the city in half. Before the line was on the railroad tracks, the counties were pretty evenly Black and White, and Edgecombe had the money. Then they made the county line the railroad tracks and something shifted in people's minds. By 2005, White people had long moved away. Pulled up stakes to Nash County, making sure their White kids went to White schools and had White friends. Edgecombe dried up. If you were White you didn't want to walk around most spots alone or you'd get the shit kicked out of you. Tre stayed out in Edgecombe with his grandmother.

Me and Brian and New had gone out there one day to try and pick him up at the house. When we were kids I'd really loved his place. His grandma made super tight breakfasts whenever I slept over. Her face was like an old love note. Warm and creased.

She'd told us he wasn't around. Out somewhere, was what she said, which was weird, because his LeBaron was in the driveway.

Whatever. We left. I didn't really feel like doing anything anyway. Me and New had been slamming Boone's Farm Blue Hawaiian the night before and I'd never been as hungover. It sucked.

"Fuck dude, I've never been this hungover before, this sucks." I said and took a long pull of Sun Drop.

I leaned my head against the passenger window of Brian's truck and watched the world. Broken down factories, decaying brick, and rusted rebar jutting out against the sky. Choked out by kudzu, overgrown with tall fescue.

"You look like shit again, my friend," New said from the back seat.

Brian jerked the wheel, and I slammed my head against the window.

"Oh fuck! I got a headache man..."

But Brian was laughing so hard he was about to lose control for real. I pulled a mashed-up pack of Pall Malls from my pocket and tried to finger out a smoke. Came up empty. I tossed the pack out the open window.

"Shit, don't do that! I'm buzzed. Had like three beers before I picked y'all up. And they'd love to pull over somebody with my profile. White cops are all over Edgecombe just waiting."

I said, "Brian, you're White."

"And White cops hate my fuckin' ass. Here."

He grabbed a pack of Newports from his cup holder and tossed it to me.

"Have one of these."

"Dude, these have like, fiberglass in them."

"Man, that's a myth. Probably. It's a free square, take it or don't."

Of course, I took it. Fiberglass or whatever, fuck it. I lit and took a deep breath. The nicotine hit my lungs and sent a shock of pleasure running through my system. My head even felt a little better.

"Minty fresh." I exhaled. "Does this count as brushing my teeth?"

He jabbed one between his grinning lips. "Yeah, you're good now."

He was about to light it when something suddenly caught New's eye.

"Shit, shit, shit. Gun."

New leaned in between us and pointed out the windshield, just ahead of us. On my side two guys were running down the sidewalk. They were going like hell, one chasing the other.

Brian slid the truck to the right, toward the curb, and slowed the car down so they were moving parallel to us. Six feet away, max. New was right. The chaser had a gun in his hand.

"Fuck. You know those guys?" I asked Brian.

"No, never seen 'em. Not my crowd," he stared until the smoke fell from his mouth.

Seeing them run on the other side of the glass, matching their speed so they stayed in the viewfinder, everything sort of felt like slow motion, like I was watching a movie, something unreal. I couldn't control it any more than I could touch it.

"What am I doing? We can't be around for whatever this is."

Brian dropped his foot on the gas and pulled away. We watched in the rearview as the prey ran up the steps to a house. He fiddled with the knob for a split second, just long enough for the dude with the gun to close the gap. He almost had the door closed when gun dude got his hand in there and blocked it.

"Fuck. Got him." Brian shook his head.

New was laughing, high and quick. "Your town is crazy! This place is an asylum. I can't believe that just happened!"

Brian whispered something to himself. "God wasn't looking out for him today."

CASPER

THE FIRST TIME GRACE and I fucked was a surprise. I was supposed to go over to her place to smoke a bowl and watch a movie while we waited for New to maybe come by and pick us up. She had mentioned *The Umbrellas of Cherbourg.*

Instead, we drank from a flask of scotch that Grace's dad kept hidden in a work bench in his garage, right next to the 1961 Jaguar he'd had refurbished. A total classic.

We put on a VHS tape of *Kids*. I'd never seen it before. She laughed at the part when the kids beat up the other kids with their skateboards while Daniel Johnston plays, then seemed embarrassed that she'd done it.

Her room was filled with books, novels from the early 20th century. Books on how to speak French. Books in French. All that paper intimidated me and made me excited.

She told me that her parents were out of town at some medical conference.

I don't really know how we ended up under the covers. We started passing the flask from opposite ends of the bed as we drew toward each other like it was inevitable, edging inch by inch until we were naked and under the heavy duvet that seemed like it used to belong to her parents.

She wouldn't let me see her body under the covers.

When I reached down to touch her I found a thicket of soft hair. I was sure it was a dark brown, but I imagined it a John Waters neon blue.

"I... I don't shave down there. I know all girls do now, but I don't. So sorry. But I'm not a little girl."

"I like it," I said. I meant it.

I hovered over her, my hard dick grazing her belly. Hesitant. Scared. I'd done this four times before with two other girls, but that didn't mean shit.

She looked me in the eye for the only time during our first encounter. "It's okay. I want it."

"I don't have a condom..." I laughed. "I didn't think this was going to happen."

"I don't care," she said.

"Oh. Okay. I don't either."

"Good. Just pull out."

She kissed me and I pressed my body against her, moved inside of her.

It was easy and natural. Like how I'd wished it had been the other times I'd done it.

She leaned her head back and closed her eyes and began to moan.

I sat up on my butt and started to fuck her like I'd seen Patrick Bateman do in front of the mirror in *American Psycho* and some porn movies so I could see her big tits move under me, pooling on her chest and sloshing up and down with me.

She moved her arm up to support her breasts as they moved, giving me a better angle.

I tried to find her eyes, but she had covered her face with a pillow. I almost stopped but she had started to moan even louder and say something. It took me a second to decipher what it was through the pillow.

"Fuck me raw," she gasped. "Fuck me raw, fuck me raw, fuck me raw."

She said it over and over again.

Before I wanted to, I said, "I'm gonna cum."

"Cum then," she said. Casual. Like, sure you can have some of my M&Ms. Cum, then.

I appreciated her so much for that. I pulled out and jettisoned a gross wad on her stomach and bush.

She laid there for a second, breathing real heavy into the pillow. It sounded like she was sucking wet cotton into her mouth. Like she was wearing a mask that had gotten yanked out of position. A luchador all turned around in the middle of the fight.

On the TV the kid from *Kids* kept saying "It's Casper" to Chloe Sevigny and I remembered hearing that he'd killed himself in a hotel in a casino a few years before we'd ended up in bed together.

"Are you... okay?" I asked.

She pulled the pillow away and smiled at me. "Yeah. That was fun."

"Oh. Oh. Cool."

She rose out of bed. Grabbed some tissues from a box on her bedside. Wiped me away. Real quick, she started trying to pull her pants on but before she could I saw the scars.

Small, sad little cuts. Surgical. Like they were made with an X-Acto. No more than an inch long. They dotted the insides of both of her thighs. Some looked fresher than others.

For a second I didn't know what to say. She saw me looking and avoided eye contact and kept pulling her pants up. She looked suddenly resigned to something and I didn't know what.

Then I said, "Come here." and pulled the blankets back a bit.

BALLS

THE SKINHEADS WERE OUT that night.

The four of them showed up in town one day and started coming to shows. Nobody knew where they came from. They ran a tattoo parlor in town, right on the edge of the railroad tracks. All of the flash tats in their window were of spiders.

Tre was playing with his other band, the Jazz Disaster at Mucho Mexico Sizzling. A local Mexican restaurant, they let creative kids do whatever in their back room. A guy who didn't know how to play saxophone was playing saxophone, while Tre hunched over a synthesizer, making it bleat like a lamb on fire. The bandage was off but I still couldn't tell what his ink was of. Dank plucked droning ambient bass underneath. Fucking sick.

I hadn't realized it but, the party at Dank's was because he'd decided to go AWOL from the Navy. He couldn't get a normal job because they'd run his social and report him, so the guy who ran Rick's Hot Dogs (Rick?) paid him less than minimum under the table to cook red hots and chili.

Dank had come back on a week-long furlough and peaced from his ship. He left because they'd promised to put him on a photography track, taking pictures of the Blue Angels, but instead stuck him peeling potatoes for a year.

Before the show, while we were drinking beers, Dank laughed when I told him I thought about writing for the Marine Corps paper.

"They're never gonna let you do that," he said. "They'll let you get shot, but they won't let you do that."

The skinheads didn't care about that. They cared that Tre was Black. They stood up at the front of the little crowd of kids and screamed at him over the noise of the Jazz Disaster.

The band stood firm. Tre grew taller behind the synth. Dank turned his bass up, an immovable force.

An empty vocal mic stood in the center of the guys, left behind by Amber Energy, the 311 cover band that had played before them. A small scene welcomes everyone they can get.

I didn't know if it was the three beers I had or the bump of crushed Percocet that I'd snorted off of New's dashboard half an hour earlier, but I felt like doing something.

I pushed through the front line and up to the mic.

"Fuck you, Nazi shit! Nazis fuck off and die!" I screamed, doing some kind of a Jello Biafra impression.

It wasn't clever, but it worked. One of the skinheads moved in.

He leaned into me. Pressed his forehead to mine. Flesh on flesh. His sweat dripped into my eyes. He screamed back into the mic.

He headbutted me but I couldn't feel it.

Just adrenaline and rage coursing through me.

Kids were screaming around us.

A hand rose above the crowd. Insistent. Panicked, even. I looked to the back of the room and saw New standing against the wall, waving me out. Fear in his bloodshot eyes. *Go. Now.*

I dropped the mic at the skinheads' feet and juked him and pushed through the tight grouping of kids and went out the side door into the warm night air. The Jazz Disaster quieted as the door fell shut behind me, locking them all away.

New hustled around the side of the building from the front exit. Brian followed behind, taking long, walking strides. Nothing was worth running over.

"We gotta go, now!" New shouted.

"What? Why?"

"Get in the car," he said.

Brian behind the wheel. Rubber burning out, tires squealing from the parking lot.

"What the fuck?" Me in the back seat.

New swiveled around from the passenger seat. "The leader, big mother fucker, bald head."

"Sounds familiar."

"Talked to me. Told me his guys were gunning for you. He couldn't protect you after your little protest anthem. They were going to kill you, my friend."

"Oh." I sat back in the seat, trying to figure out how it felt to have someone really want me dead. Proud, I decided.

"Whooo!" New let out a yelp and pumped his fist out the open window. "That shit was fucking crazy! Fucking insane. Allan, you should be proud of your level of insanity."

Brian laughed.

New smiled at me in the rear-view mirror. "I'm liking you more and more," he said.

For a night, I was brave and strong. I was wired hot. I never wanted to sleep again.

"Where are we going?" I asked.

"You ain't gotta show ID at Sharks n' Shooters. They'll serve anybody," Brian offered. He almost swerved off the road as he took his hands off the wheel to light a cigarette.

New grabbed the wheel and steadied us. Brian nodded his thanks.

"I got a place we can go," I said.

"Then let's go," New said.

He turned up the stereo and blasted Charles Bronson and we rode on into the darkness.

There were still pews, nailed into the floor over molding, shredded carpet. Walls of wooden slats slumped around us. The podium at the head of it all, and the cross that must have hung behind it, were long gone.

Brian laid on one of the pews, head hanging off the end. He held a forty over his head and tried to pour it into his mouth. It doused his face.

New stood in the center of the pews, practicing kung fu with a cigarette hanging from his lips. He laughed at Brian. "You're waterboarding yourself."

"Fucking Cheney..." Brian muttered. Then, to me, "You were fucking funny as shit up there tonight man, I've never in my life seen something that crazy. Balls out. You should be in a band or something."

"Nah, I'm too scared to do it when I'm not fucked up. It's not like, uh, sustainable."

New said, "You seen that 9/11 thing, that *Loose Change* doc? Shit's fucked up. We're so fucked."

We'd snorted another line of Percs in the car. Good and loose. I cradled my forty like a baby in my arms.

"Jack Kerouac used to go to this church." My voice ricocheted off the walls of the dying room. "He lived with his sister for a while in Rocky Mount and he'd walk six miles each way every Sunday to get here. He was weirdly into God."

"Jack who?" Brian asked.

New laughed at him and Brian looked away.

"Jack Kerouac. It's a poet," I said. "I'll get you a book."

"Kerouac-off."

New doubled over laughing and Brian smiled a private little smile, happy with his wordplay.

I turned the forty up and drained it.

"Fuck this place," I said.

I took my dick out and pissed into the old carpet. It felt good to just have my dick out in the air. I was happy to be a man.

The guys watched and laughed as I emptied myself onto the floor. All the beer and Mountain Dew Live Wire and molecular traces of opioids pooled around my feet. Rusty.

I zipped up and chucked my empty forty through the window, shattering it.

"Fuck this place," New giggled and picked up a stone from the floor and threw it into another window.

Glass went flying and I smiled.

HELP

"LISTENING TO YOU NOW, it sounds like you do a lot of impulsive things."

I shifted in the fake leather chair across from the doctor woman that my dad's insurance could pay for. I kept hard eye contact with her. I was trying to intimidate her. I didn't know why.

She smiled at me. *Patience is a virtue.*

"It sounds like you have a lot of emotional ups and downs. One minute you're feeling good about yourself. The next, you're not. One second you hate the world, the next you're in love. Does that sound right?"

"I don't know." I shrugged. "I guess so."

"That's really interesting."

She let it hang there and looked at me for a long time. The framed degrees and awards on the wall loomed over me.

"Well. I think you might be bi-polar. What do you think about that, Allan?"

Kept my face tight. Show no fear. "I've never been, like, manic before. Like buying every pair of pants in the store and shit."

"A lot of people with bi-polar disorder don't experience mania," she said.

"Oh."

"I can refer you to a psychiatrist who can help get you on a prescription drug plan. Probably Wellbutrin. That will help with the smoking too if you want to do that. You smell like cigarette smoke. I'd like to see you again as well if you would be open to that."

"I don't really want to be medicated. All doped up, like that. I don't need that. Or this."

She wrote something down. Added a period at the end, *hard*.

"That's fine, Allan. Help is there if you decide you need it. I think at some point you will realize that you do."

CARDINAL

EVERCLEAR WENT DOWN SWEET with the Cheerwine. The taste of Carolina.

"I know it's redneck shit, but it's so beautiful out here. It's like- Oh, damn it."

Tre pulled his foot out of the river and stumbled back, jamming his fishing pole into the mud.

"I can't believe we're fishing," I said.

We hadn't fished since we were little kids when Tre's dad was still alive. Something had drawn us out to the river that day. I was glad for it. The warmth of the sun, the sound of the water, the Everclear. It was comforting.

"I can't believe I'm kinda drunk already."

He wandered back from the water and slumped back into a folding chair under the shade of a hickory tree. The mesh webbing sagged under him. The rusting metal creaked. Something comforting about the sounds. He pulled a PBR out of the cooler and shook the ice water off his hand.

"Ahh, cold burns just right. Can't do the Cheerwine anymore. Too sweet."

"I like Nehi," I offered. "But the Cheerwine isn't bad."

"Nehi? Fuck that shit. Pabst Blue Ribbon!" He yelled until he ran out of breath. "Man, I am drunk. Cheerwine, that's pretty funny."

I drained my Cheerwine, dropped it in the grass. *I'll get it later.* I walked over and dropped down into the chair next to him. "Gimme a Peeber." He flipped me a beer.

"For going fishing, we're not doing a lotta fishing."

I cracked the beer. "Dude, I'm sitting in a chair by the beautiful, dirty Tar River, getting drunk with my probably oldest friend. I am fishing."

"Oh, shit. That's right."

I checked out his neck. The tattoo looked like a bird. I couldn't tell what kind. It was pretty realistic, its wings all spread out like it was soaring through the air.

"I gotta ask man..." I was drunk enough to do the unthinkable: question someone's neck tattoo. "What's up with the neck tat?"

"I got it done at that place down by the old mall."

"The one down by the Holiday Inn?"

"Nah, the one by the highway. Down halfway to Tarboro."

"Oh, that one. Ew, fuck. Why?"

"'Cause dude, they're still in business against all the odds. That says a lot about their work, right? I walked in and they asked me what artist I wanted, and I found this wall-eyed guy in the back. He looked like Cheetah Chrome got hit in the head with a claw hammer. Like, he couldn't find the horizon with either eye."

"What in the fuck..."

Something in that moment made us both spontaneously start laughing until he caught a breath and said, "It makes sense. Like the shop, if he's working there he must be *really* good. And I was right. Right?"

"Is that like... that's a bird, right? That's a bird."

"Don't be an asshole. It's a cardinal. North Carolina state bird."

I didn't even know that was a thing and I told him so.

He said, "I have to have something to remember this place by when I leave it. What are you gonna remember?"

I watched the river go by and thought about throwing my line back in, but I didn't.

SHINY

FROM THE ROOF OF Grace's parent's house, you couldn't see much. A strip mall. A Chinese restaurant that had closed down. Roads that circled around and around, going nowhere.

At least the houses were nicer. Her dad was making that doctor money. The houses were older and made out of real things, brick and wood, not skinned in vinyl siding like my parent's.

Grace was drawing on her shoes with a sharpie, filling in the dirty white spots of her Chuck Taylor's. Everybody in the scene had them. The boots for our uniform. Had to be the high tops or you were a poseur. Commit to the laces, goddammit. She finished up and held her foot in the air to show me. It was a little black heart, broken in half with jagged lines, drawn over her big toe. She smiled, pleased with herself.

She took a drink from a big plastic cup we'd pulled from the kitchen. It had her mom's initials on it in the curly-cue font. SKL. We'd filled it with rum we stole from her dad and Diet Coke we'd stolen from SKL. Grace said she didn't know which they would be more angry about. She sipped again and winced from the rum, sucking her teeth. She handed me the cup.

She didn't know it, but I'd taken half a Vic in the car before I'd gone inside, and I was feeling real good and warm. Safe with her. I hoped she wouldn't know. Not because I was hiding it, really. Just because I didn't have any more to share. Any stoned effect she might be catching from me I figured would be explained by the alcohol.

I took a drink and forced myself not to react to the taste in front of her. I read the cup. "S-K-L. Skull. Your mom is cool."

"She's not cool. I promise. I'm gonna write some lyrics on your Chucks, 'kay?"

"As long as it's not like Dashboard or something."

"Jesus. You know me."

She crawled down the roof a bit and knelt down over my shoe with the Sharpie open in her hand, eyes wide with the possibilities.

While she worked, I listened to the music coming through her window. Wilco playing "Jesus, Etc." I hadn't liked them much before that record came out. Too folky and country. Like pickin' n grinnin'. But that album, that song. They were perfect. *Summerteeth* had been pretty good too, "She's a Jar" and all that, but they'd gotten fucked up after they kicked out Jay Bennett, the guy behind the control board. The perfect sideman. The record after *Foxtrot* was obnoxious.

She crawled up next to me, sat thigh to thigh. She hooked her left leg around my right and nestled her foot up against mine, her arch fitting perfectly against the part where my toes began; the two Chucks coming together like a couple, spooning.

"Bread and butter," she said.

"What?"

"They go together."

I kissed the top of her head. Roots were showing from where the red was growing out, revealing the dark hair underneath, her true self creeping out. I kissed it again. I ran my fingers down her arm to find her hand. I snagged a thick leather bracelet on her wrist and accidentally pulled it down. Three small cuts lived underneath it. They were fresh. She hurriedly pulled the bracelet back up to cover them.

There was something strange in the air then, something sad. Something scary in a slow, creeping sort of way. It hovered there between us.

Finally, she said, "I couldn't explain it if I tried."

I held her hand.

"What did you write?"

"Hold me fast. It's lyrics from "La Vie en Rose." Not the original French one, the Louis Armstrong version that-"

I laughed and said, "I get you."

We leaned back against the warm, red brick of her house. The sun was going down, the kind of sun you saw in movies when it was supposed to be just the right moment. The Perc and the rum coming together inside me made the world glow even more. Beautiful. Streams of gold broke through the gaps in the rooftops of suburban houses. Like the sun was an egg that

God cracked over our town so that all the golden yolk could spread out and hold us. She took another sip from the plastic cup, sucked her teeth, and handed it to me.

"It's sweet, the Coke and rum."

"Yeah." I took a big drink, and it was sweet, and it felt like the sun had lowered down into my belly and was shining a light all through me.

I put my arm around her. Pulled her tight. Took a deep breath of fresh air. It smelled like sweat and lawn clippings and I didn't know what would happen to us or that four years on from when we were sitting on that roof, in 2009, Jay Bennett would die from a fentanyl overdose, but everything just felt so, so good I really thought I had figured something out.

BUSTED

THE LEPER'S ARM FELL off. When the blonde, naked peasant woman bent over to pick it up she discovered the fingers had been frozen with the middle, index, and pinky sticking out in rigor mortis. The shocker. She rolled back in the hay, spreading her legs while the two lepers watched.

"Oh my god!" Grace giggled and closed her eyes.

Kelly said, "This is fucking unbelievable. This is a porn movie? I can't believe this."

"It's called the *Days of Whore*," New said proudly. "I think there's a scene later with Jesus."

The woman slowly, passionately, moved the hand in and out of her. White-knuckling the dead forearm, her moans filling the living room of the trailer Brian lived alone in. I wondered if the animals in the woods around us could hear. And his neighbors. Four mobile homes lay in a field at uneven distances along a gravel horseshoe that left and then returned to the state highway. Brian's was the second in the line. I pictured them all, the humans and animals, stopping whatever they were doing and listening in shock to the full color sin on the TV.

I also wondered where Brian's family had gone. There were pictures on the wall, a room with dresses hanging in the closet that I'd found while creeping around once, but he never explained where everyone in his life had gone.

"You jerk off to this don't you? Be honest." Kelly threw the TV remote at New.

He caught it. *Nice.* "Fuck no. This is my brother's, I stole it. I don't know how he enjoys this. He has autism though, so, I dunno."

"Oh dawg, I'm sorry." Brian put his hand on New's shoulder.

"This is actually pretty awesome," Tre said begrudgingly.

Tre was there too. But he didn't seem to want to be.

Grace moved closer to me, pulling the blanket we had over our legs tighter. Somehow we'd become a couple without discussing it. Fine with me. The peasant lady got down on her hands and knees. Oozing leppers slid their erect cocks into her.

A phone went off somewhere in the room. "Oh shit, I got a text," Brian said. He rummaged around under old food boxes and bills until he found his phone and flipped it open. "Oh shit, oh shit. Y'all know Wesley Avent?"

Everybody in the room shrugged. He looked at New.

"Why're you looking at me? I'm not from here, everyone I know is in this room right now."

"Yeah, well, he's dead. He was at Good Tymes, and he bumped into this gangbanger and spilled a drink on him, and the dude straight up shot him in the parking lot."

"Gangbanger?" Kelly asked. "What does that mean?"

"It means he happened to not be of the Caucasian persuasion. That politically correct enough? Dude's dead."

Under the blanket my hand found Grace's thigh just above the knee and I gripped it tightly, feeling her torn blue pantyhose, bright as neon, moving up her leg to the hem of her unfinished jean miniskirt. I had taken a Vyvanse earlier and I felt cored out and edgy, dirty and vacant inside, horny as fuck.

I whispered something to her. Got up and went down the little hallway to the bathroom. Sat on the toilet with my pants up but left the door unlocked. The Vyvanse triggered my brain on the toilet, and I immediately had to shit like crazy. Sharp pains in my stomach had me doubling over when Grace came in. The pains went away. I locked the door, and I pushed her against the wall, and I pawed at her tits. I picked her up and sat her ass in the sink. Pulled her tights down and got on my knees, ate her pussy until it sounded like the counter was going to rip out of the drywall. She couldn't stop giggling. She got up and bent over the toilet, bracing herself against the tank with her hands. I pulled her skirt up over her ass and fucked her. She moaned and every time she did it had this little edge to it like *I can't believe I'm doing this*. I fucked her until I couldn't anymore. I pulled out and shot a load between her thighs into the toilet water.

I came out first and sat on the couch. I looked around for New or Brian to see if they'd give me a sly nod of approval, but they were gone. It was just Tre, Kelly, and Mohammed, who seemed to be passed out in a raggedy old papasan. Nobody looked at me weird but that just made me feel like they were avoiding looking at me because they knew. A couple minutes later Grace came back. She sat next to me, and we held hands tightly.

On the TV one of the leper's dicks ripped off while he was fucking the maiden. He stepped back in horror and sadness, looking at his dismembered member as it pulsed on the ground.

"Somebody read *Naked Lunch,"* Grace smirked.

I didn't get it, but I squeezed her hand like I did.

"These special FX are honestly pretty good," Kelly said.

A sliding glass door opened and New walked in. "How's the porn?"

"Not bad," Kelly said. "The special FX are pretty good, honestly."

"Where's Brian?" someone asked.

"Dunno. I went out to take a piss and then wandered around, just looking at these beautiful stars and constellations and shit." New stepped close to the TV, obstructing our view. He watched while the girl, continuing to get fucked from behind by the armless leper, picked up the other leper's still-stiff lost cock and start sucking it off. "I like the message of this movie. Even if you're a leper, don't let it keep you down. Keep fuckin'. You just gotta live until you're dead."

"Profound," Tre said.

“I like it.” I upended my beer and drank. “Live ‘til you’re dead.”

“Did you hear what happened to Ángel?” Tre asked.

I didn’t know who he was talking about. “No.”

“He worked at Mucho Mexico. He was a senior at Northern. After you guys left the other night those Nazi fucks were so pissed off they didn’t get to kick Allan’s ass, they waited around until the restaurant closed and grabbed Ángel when he took out some garbage bags. They curb stomped him. Almost killed him.”

Nobody said anything.

“You went to Northern, didn’t you Allan? He was just below you.”

A year below me. I didn’t even know who he was. My stomach was all knotted up. I leaned forward and did half a line off the table, hoping it was Vicodin or Percocet. Something to bring me down a bit and sand the edges away.

“That’s awful,” Grace said. “That’s so awful.”

Tre pointed at me. “Your nose is bleeding.”

The severed cock busted into the girl’s mouth.

FEELINGS

THE GREAT THING ABOUT pills is that they make you feel so fucking good and require so little of you to get them in your blood, especially if you're one of the lucky few like me who doesn't get sick from them.

Why put a needle in your arm? Why suffer coughing fits from smoking something? Don't like the taste of alcohol? Great, pharmaceuticals can be washed down with a little water and don't even touch your tongue while they do it.

In our case, it was easy as hell to get too. And, unbelievably, free. Brian was an angel sent from opioid heaven, someone willing to spread the wealth to those he liked in exchange for nothing more than decent company. And there was a lot of wealth to go around. Because of his well-documented migraines, couldn't-give-a-shit doctors, and a general ignorance about how addictively *good* good could feel, he was working with, from what I could count, around six different prescriptions at once. Of course, those were just for pain management. There were also the "study" drugs that jacked you up like a trucker from the 60's or a housewife in the

50's, the anti-anxiety meds that he also probably needed but had consciously lied to a psychiatrist to get, the mood-stabilizers, the muscle relaxers, and on and on and on and on and on and on.

My favorite, everyone's favorite, were the pain destroyers. Little bits of heaven that could make your entire life feel like it had meaning. That your brain was floating in a void of gummy worm dreams. That everything was possible for you. It was all just beyond the horizon, and you'd be there eventually, and it was all so certain that there was no need to rush or stress. Your life was going to be incredible very, very soon because you were you and you were special.

There are a few ways to take them. You can just swallow them like their farm team cousins Advil. You can parachute them, where you'd empty the contents of a gel cap into a thin piece of paper, wrap it up, and swallow it. The paper broke down faster into your system, supposedly getting around time release effects from the manufacturer. You can crush them up and snort them, probably my favorite. I liked the group ritual of it all, everyone hovering over the table together, deciding who's suspended driver's license would be used to crush our love into thin white lines of powder. I can't prove this but putting it up my nose made it feel like I was getting it that much more quickly into my brain.

They're all a little different and special in their own ways.

Percocet was a good friend at parties. It's got oxycodone in it, but it's cut with acetaminophen, so it's not as intense. You'd feel a nice mellow body and mind high, something that takes the edge off of the entire world, making everything velvety smooth, but you wouldn't get your ass tranqued out. You can drink on it without worrying. You could even fuck around and do more than one and not worry about ending up in an ambulance. I liked Percocet.

Codeine is cool. Kinda like Perc grew some muscles. Hard to be mad at that. But liquid codeine...that was the shit. So hard to get. Mix it up with some juice or soda, get some lean going. Lean 'cause you're gonna be fucking leaning. Ha ha. It's syrupy and a little sweet and medicine-y in a way that will bring you back to when you were a kid and all you wanted to do was eat purple flavored Dimetapp like candy. You gotta be careful with the liquid though. It's easy to get weird with your own measurements and overdo it.

Vicodin is really cool.

OxyContin is not something to fuck with but fuck with it. It's a couch drug. You won't want to talk, and you won't need to. You can just telepathically communicate to whoever you're sitting next to, so you'll save time that way too. The quickest way to know that everything is okay in your life is to pop an Oxy. Don't go for more than one though, especially if you're starting out. You might even want to split one of these bad boys up with a good friend.

Morphine is it. Straight from the poppy. The closest thing you can get to heroin. Morphine is everything. You will never feel better than this without putting a needle in your vein. Take all of it that you can when you can. You won't even care if you die. It's all God's plan and God is right there in your belly.

In the end, no matter how much or what kind you take, you will want more. You will be simultaneously scared at how much you want more and how awesome you are becoming once it hits your system.

If you get out and quit taking them, you will spend your life remembering how good it felt and underplaying how much you were willing to give up for that feeling when the epidemic comes up in casual conversations. You will tell people you had a good time, but you weren't a statistic.

You will be old, and you will dream poppy-fueled dreams, remembering how good it felt to be a friend with someone who's name you can't remember.

Almost a million people will have partied just as hard and felt as good as you have, but they will not be able to look back. They will be dead. Killed by the party.

You, though, you will remember.

CLEAN

MOHAMMED HAD CALLED BRIAN in the afternoon. His voice on the other end was frail, scratchy. Like a scarecrow came to life. It sounded like he had just stopped crying or was about to start. I don't think he knew he was on speaker phone.

"The panic is here, man," he said. "I need help. I need medicine."

Brian took him off speaker and put his phone to his ear.

"It's bad today?" he asked.

"Welcome to Taco Bell, can I take your order?" said a woman from the other end of the drive thru speaker.

"Fuck me. Yo, Mo, hold on a sec dawg. Sorry." He put the car in park and leaned out the window to the speaker. "Lemme get a, uh...lemme get one of them Mexican Pizzas."

"The meal or just the pizza?"

"I didn't say meal did I?"

An exasperated sigh. "No. Anything else?"

Brian turned to New next to him and then me in the backseat. He gestured, annoyed. *Come on*.

I said, "I'll try one of those Grilled Stuft Burritos. Steak. Oh, and a soft taco."

"Jesus, Allan. Just a Diet Coke for me, Brian. Thanks."

Brian turned back to the speaker woman. "Grilled Stuft Burrito, Diet Coke."

"Oh, and the soft-"

"Your total is nine dollars and-"

But Brian was already pulling forward.

"You call the VA?" he asked into the phone. "...Dawg, I got you. For sure. ...You ain't paying for shit, man. Get outta here with that mess. 'Sides, I know your broke ass ain't got a nickel anyways." He laughed. "We'll be over in ten..." he looked at the line of cars in front of us. "Twenty minutes."

I was halfway done with the burrito by the time we got to Mohammed's house in the dead end of a cul-de-sac at the ass end of a new housing development. Cookie cutter models that repeated every three houses. Vinyl siding, cement porches out front. Dirt patches spotted every lawn. The owners were too busy working to afford the house to actually maintain it, so they already looked threadbare. Like they smelled like cat piss inside.

We piled out of the car and onto Mohammed's decaying lawn. Brian gave New and I little side looks, like *what are you doing stay in the car,* but we didn't want to stay in the car, and he didn't say anything, so we followed him up to the front door. Brian knocked.

His phone dinged. A text message. He flipped it open and read aloud, haltingly.

"Come in. I'm upstairs." he closed the phone. "He says come in, he's upstairs."

"...yeah," New said.

Brian opened the door and New and I moved inside like we were taking the first step onto an alien planet. Brian whispered to us.

"Y'all stay down here. Be quiet."

He moved up the stairs with delicate footing, careful not to make a sound. He disappeared and New and I took in the room. I was expecting some kind of chaos, but it was completely in order. Like, supreme order. The room looked like it had been staged for the Rent-A-Center catalog. Cheap furniture, perfectly matched, perfectly clean. Not a speck of dust. Not a single piece of artwork or family photographs.

I was suddenly ashamed that I'd wanted to come inside, to invade his psychosis. It was the most depressing room I'd ever been in, and I wanted to crawl inside myself. Instead, I unwrapped my burrito and took a bite.

"You brought that in with you?" New looked at me like I was an animal. He turned his disgust to the room, gesturing around. In a voice that seemed a little too loud he said, "This place sucks. I thought he was gonna be going apeshit."

That hung in the air for a moment before he course corrected. "That sounded really bad. I didn't mean it like that."

Through a mouth of beans I said, "Brian's a really nice guy. I don't think I knew that. He's like, actually nice. Just *nice*, you know what I mean? Like he's good."

New considered this information. “Hm. I guess so. I hadn’t noticed either.” Then he asked, “What’s his real name?”

“I thought it was Brian...”

“No butt plug, Mohammed. What’s his real name?”

“Oh yeah, he told me it was a stupid nickname, but I don’t know,” I said. I hadn’t asked him.

I finished my burrito and considered throwing it away in his trash can but that seemed like an affront, a sin against Mohammed, so I wadded up the wrapper and stuffed it into my pocket.

New creeped over to the base of the stairs and listened. Nothing. He grinned at me like John Belushi peeping on some girls. He took a step up the stairs. The step creaked and he paused. When nothing happened, he took another one.

“Don’t go up there,” I whispered.

“This is boring me to death. I would like to know what’s going on, Allan,” he said.

“Stop,” I hissed.

He rolled his eyes. He knew I wouldn’t actually stop him. He took another step and then we heard it from upstairs: something flying across the room, a lamp or something, and crashing against a wall. Mohammed yelling in low, frightened tones. Brian speaking to him firmly, softly. All of it unintelligible. And then we heard Mohammed making loud, guttural barks. We couldn’t tell if he was crying or laughing.

DEFER

THE BOWL FULL OF brown steamed in front of me. Grace's eyes locked on me. Anticipation.

On one side of me stood a massive china cabinet filled with what looked like super expensive plates and glasses. Crystal and stuff. On the other side was a giant painting of a deer. The deer had huge horns branching out from its head and angry black eyes. Everything in the room was dark wood and forest greens. She sat across the antique table from me, watching.

It felt like a test. Or a trap. I wanted to run, but I trusted her.

"So... it's just like, onions?" I asked.

"It's French onion soup," she said.

"But all that's in there is like, a lot of onions?"

"And broth and cheese on top," she said.

Grace pushed it closer to me. Nodded at the spoon beside me. She said, "You like cheese."

"Yeah... Yeah. I like onions too. I just wanted to make sure it was just onions. Didn't want any surprises."

Water sprayed and pots banged in the kitchen. Her mom had offered to clean up after Grace had made the soup. No fighting or anything, just offered, like a chump. She was whistling something in there, all happy, sounding like KC and the Sunshine band, some shit, and I resented her even though she had been nice to me when she opened the door and didn't even tell us we had to keep Grace's bedroom door open, though we did anyway since her dad was home.

"Hey shortcake," said her dad from the doorway of the dining room. He smiled at her, avoiding me. *Just checking in on your loser boyfriend!*

"Hi, Dad." Grace waved to him.

"Hi, Dr. Byrne," I said, all smiles.

"Allan," he said. Then added, "It's Allan, right?"

He'd heard my name a dozen times before. Fucking asshole. I wondered if he knew I fucked his daughter in a trailer bathroom.

He came into the room and stood on the other side of the table, across from us. An oil painting hung behind him. A hunting dog was chomping down onto the throat of a goose. The bird was screaming, and blood was pouring out, like more blood than I thought people who made oil paintings were allowed to put in there unless it was Jesus. Dad had a sharp jawline and a brush cut. His arms were kind of jacked. He definitely had that dad strength that could chop down a tree or kick your ass for not using a condom.

"Dad, I told you. Yes. Jesus."

"Allan, not Jesus." I was trying for a laugh but got nothing out of him.

He had a good, solid, doctor posture. Very American shoulders. The New Colossus. He tossed a thick envelope onto the table. It had a picture of multicultural youths sitting in the grass with a university building in the background. They were laughing and reading from textbooks at the same time for some reason. Above them, in big letters, it said Sarah Lawrence College.

"This came in the mail. I think it's got your roommate info in it."

"Oh, cool." Grace didn't pick it up. Didn't give him anything to continue the conversation with. We waited for him to leave.

Instead, he said, "You're gonna get a weirdo because you deferred like this. I told you; you defer for a semester like this, you're gonna get stuck living with some weirdo that nobody else wanted."

I was staring down at the dining room table so I couldn't see him, but it felt like he was talking at me.

Her mom spoke up from the kitchen with a light Southern lilt. "She wanted to hang out with her friends a little bit before going away! They're not going to see each other again hardly ever after all this."

The statement hung in the air. The dad nodded along. Grace didn't protest. I pointed to one of the kids on the envelope. An Asian girl, giggling over a calculus textbook.

"Why's the Asian kid gotta be doing math? Kinda racist, right?"

For a moment they both stared at me. The mom laughed in the kitchen.

"Get in touch with the roommate okay, kiddo? See if you guys need a fridge or a TV or something."

"Okay, thanks Dad."

He was gone and we were alone and struggling for something to say, which hadn't been a problem for us before. The soup was getting cold in front of me. The cheese looked all rubbery.

"Sarah Lawrence. Isn't that in New Jersey?"

"New York, actually. In the city."

"Far away," I said.

"Far away," she said.

"Right now, you're here."

"Right now, I'm here."

She reached out and took my hand. I felt uncomfortable in the silence and said, "Those student loans, huh? Must be crazy." Sounding like a dad myself.

Her face scrunched up in mock embarrassment. Awkward. "I uh, I don't have any student loans. I'm lucky. I got a scholarship to fill in some of it and then-"

"It's okay," I said. "That's awesome. Take that money, use it. You're lucky. That's good."

"Thanks. Sometimes people get weird about it, you know..."

"Ah, fuck 'em."

I tried the soup beneath the thick slab of lukewarm cheese. There were a lot of onions.

"I like it," I said, not totally lying but sounding like I was.

She rolled her eyes a little. Said, "Je ne te crois pas, mais merci."

I didn't know what the hell she'd just said, but I was so impressed with her that I sort of couldn't believe I was sitting at the table. *Who let me in here?*

"Holy shit. You speak French?"

MASK

THE SHOTGUN LIT UP and kicked back into my shoulder. The little ceramic disc arced safely through the air. No worries. It shattered when it hit a rock and died.

"Balls."

I cracked open the gun. Pop, pop. Shells flew out the back and landed in the dirt. I handed the shotgun to my dad.

"That's alright. Get the next one."

My shoulder was killing me. I didn't mind, I had a Vic in my pocket that Brian had given me, and I'd pop it once the gun was put away.

Dad loaded it up and stepped into position. I took the remote.

"Ready?" he asked. I nodded. "Pull!"

I pulled and the machine whipped two discs into the air, one from the left, one from the right. Bang. Bang. They exploded, spreading their shattered bones against thin wisps of clouds.

Silence on the drive back. Out the window crop fields went past. Once filled with cotton and tobacco. Now it was harvested soil and stems, dying as the fall approached. Soon they'd be frosted over.

"Mom says your therapy is going well."

I had lied a week before about continuing to see the lady in her little room with the fake leather. Evidently they hadn't gotten an insurance bill back.

"Yeah," I said. "It's going great. Like I'm learning a lot. About myself."

"That's good," he said.

We passed by an old, sagging house in the middle of a field, about thirty yards back from the road. White paint chipping off its sides. Second floor windows angled like angry eyes cut into a jack-o-lantern. A tattered Confederate flag hung limp above the steps. A few pickup trucks and a beat-up motorcycle stood in the gravel around the house.

Rumor said it was a hangout spot for the local Klan chapter. There was no reason to think that wasn't true. The fact that it was a total shithole seemed good enough evidence. Dad put a little speed on as we drove past.

"Can I give you some wisdom son?" I didn't respond. He plowed ahead anyway. "If you ever find yourself doing something you've got to wear a mask for, take a step back. You shouldn't ever have to hide your face."

"The doctor woman thinks I might be bi-polar," I said. I added, "But I don't think so."

"Oh." He didn't know what to say and I felt bad for putting him in a position where he had to find the words. "Well, you know your mom might also have a, uh- I shouldn't talk about that behind her back. It's good you're looking into it, son. That's good."

"Can I ask you something?"

"Sure, shoot."

"Why did you retire here? We're not from here. We could have gone anywhere. Like, why here?"

He drummed his fingers on the steering wheel, awkwardly playing along to a song on the radio. I think it was Dokken. He knew it well.

"Honestly, I don't know. I mean, you know, your mom and me are from Macon, we knew we wanted to end up back around this area. The post office job was here, and your mom liked the house well enough and so we just stayed. I... I guess, yeah, I don't really know. It just kinda happened."

He said it like he was realizing it for the first time.

I said, "Yeah. That makes sense. I get that, actually."

His brows furrowed and he frowned a little bit. He turned the Dokken up but kept his hands tight on the wheel.

We moved into town proper, and the world whipped by. Walmart, Texas Steakhouse, Kmart, gas station, gas station, Bojangles, Cook Out, Hardee's, Walmart. All the choices, becoming a blur of nothing.

LIMEWIRE

ME, BRIAN, NEW, KELLY, and Grace all parachuted Adderall before we went to Gator's where we drank and drank, like too many beers to remember, but everybody was so cool that night and the lights were so warm I just felt like I could be anything and that all of these people were my friends and that tomorrow was going to be a really good day so of course I wasn't going to stop drinking and nobody else was either but the Adderall was time release and I felt like I wasn't getting anything, like it wasn't *releasing* inside me so I talked Brian or somebody into giving me another one and then the world just ignited, my pulse going crazy until the pulse felt plural and overall I was just sweaty as fuck, inside and out, and Grace and I kept holding hands under the table and New kept making fun of us but we didn't care and we got into really deep conversations about what the thing of it is and what the thing of it was and just, like, the thing of it all, talking, talking, talking until the bar was closing at which point we all got pretty fucking bummed out, but then this big blonde lady who was pretty good looking, grown up good on white bread, collards, scrapple, et al., who had been dancing on the bar with her very large breasts out only minutes before said "Fuck this, the party ain't ending, we're getting a room at the Microtel across the road", so everybody drove across over there and we got two adjoining rooms and kept the party going and shit got crazy to the point where the well-fed blonde is getting double teamed on a mattress by a White guy and a Black guy and she was actually cumming so hard she was squirting everywhere, like on a LimeWire vid, and Grace and Kelly and I sat there and watched them fuck rough with some other folks I didn't really know and New walked into the room and watched for a minute and said, "Chess board, *nice*" and the Black guy who was fucking her ass at the time grabbed the TV remote and flung it across the room and it hit New in the eye and it was probably because the blood in my veins was rushing so fast that my brain kinda short circuited and I laughed about that until I was actually crying while, of course, nobody else paid any attention cause they were watching the threeway and getting horny, at least, Grace and I got really boned up because we ended up actually fucking on the floor on a pile of sheets next to the actual bed so that we were all just moaning and sweating together while everyone watched, with Grace's big tits spilling out from her Camper Van Beethoven shirt pulled up to her neck, though the pillow over her face was kinda weird, but she was so into it, so fucking wet and moaning so hard into the dirty pillow that everybody still enjoyed watching, which really escalated when Kelly pulled the pillow back and kissed Grace deep, with Grace kissing her back, so Kelly sucked on Grace's nipples and everyone cheered and I felt like a fucking god until this shithead who's name I don't know I guess felt like he could be Kelly and reached out, grabbing Grace's tit and shaking it around like Indiana Jones testing the weight before stealing an artifact, so I punched him while still fucking her which made everybody else but him get amped up (at this point even the White guy from the threesome was watching us fuck) and after I hit him Grace's eyes lit up red, she went nuts, she pushed me on my back and sat on my cock and just started slamming down on me again and again until all the whiskey and the adrenaline and the attention and all the all the all the speed just hit hit hit and I didn't even pull out I just came inside of her for what felt like a lifetime while people laughed or whooped or walked away 'cause that's all folks, so Grace got up and flopped down on her back on the bed next to the blonde girl and the Black guy who were still going for gold and she just laid there on her back while all that stuff that was in me ran out of her, onto her thighs and the bed, and while I watched her lay there, pink and exhausted, I realized that she might feel weird about showing her face but deep down she wanted to show the world everything and she would, this realization made me feel like my heart was going to explode or maybe that was the speed so I got another beer and walked around and talked to people and nobody seemed to care that all that Adderall had flowed to my dick and I had a full on boner until morning when everybody felt shame seeping in from the oozing tendrils of the sun and we all admitted defeat and everyone put their clothes on and Grace and I waited down in the parking lot chain smoking cigarettes, so that Brian could help the blonde girl find her bra and get herself together so that he could drive her back to her car by 7am so that she could pick her kids up from their dad's place in time to get them to school.

LIGHTS

I'D HAD TO PISS for the last half hour but everything else felt so good I didn't want to move from the couch. Also, every bone in me felt like it was a million pounds of soft bread. But eventually I decided that it was either lay there in Brian's living room feeling good while the DVD menu to a Suicide Girls burlesque show played over and over again until I pissed myself all over his couch or just get up.

I got up. Fresh air sounded okay, and I figured I'd kill two birds by pissing out in Brian's backyard. He probably wouldn't mind. I think I'd seen him do a shit out there before. I couldn't remember where the back door was. In the kitchen Mohammed was standing at the counter spreading creamy peanut butter on white bread. He'd been digging deep to get the dregs out of an industrial sized plastic jar and his hands were smeared with peanut butter.

"Yo..." I said. "Where's the door to the outside?"

Mohammed wordlessly pointed to the two double-sided glass doors about four feet to my left. The ones I'd gone through a million times before.

“Shit. Thanks.”

“Hey.”

Mohammed licked peanut butter off the back of his hand like a cat. He licked his fingers and reached into a jar of pickles. Spitty, peanuty fingers grabbed a pickle spear, then another, then a third and laid them, one by one, down onto their butter bed.

“Yeah?” I asked, sharper than I’d meant to. I liked Mohammed but I didn’t have time for whatever this shit was. I really had to pee.

“Huh? Oh. I wanted to say thank you. For that time a while back, when you guys came by.” He dropped the other piece of slathered bread on top and mashed his fist down on the pile. Raw power. “That was cool.”

“Oh, yeah, for sure. But honestly I didn’t do anything, you know? I was just with Brian.”

“Yeah,” he chewed thoughtfully and talked through peanut butter. “But I feel like you would have come if I had your phone number.”

“I think I would have, Mo.”

“My mom used to make this sandwich when she was pregnant with me. That and peach Nehi. Drank so much of that junk she can’t stand the taste today.”

I wondered what my mom drank while she was pregnant with me.

He pulled the sleeve of his t-shirt up to show bright burn marks on his upper bicep. So pink they still looked hot.

"Brian did it last night. We were doing knife hits off the stovetop and he branded me. It's a cross."

I didn't say anything.

"I asked him to," he said.

"I didn't know you were into God," I said, forgetting for a second that I was about to go into septic shock.

"Oh, no. I'm a pagan, brother. Full on. But my family took me to church every Sunday. Southern Baptist. My mom and grandma especially, they were *into it*. But they were also doing some weird stuff, you know? Painting the ceiling of the porch bright blue to keep away spirits and all that. Nowadays my mom would probably be called a witch to some people.

I loved going to church with them. Singing and getting dressed up and getting Krispy Kreme after. So this symbol, the cross, it still means something good to me.

It's something to help me remember all the good moments. Doing knife hits with your buddy. Eating a sandwich. Being in love with somebody. The other stuff that just sucks, it'll fucking stomp you. Stomp you into the dirt, man. So mark the good shit down when you can.

It's my guiding light. When I forget I can look down at the cross and remember to follow it. The good stuff."

He winked at me and took a bite out of the sandwich.

I wandered outside and the chill night air reminded me that I was alive, and I was grateful for it. I tried to think of something to get tattooed on me to lead me forward. Came up with nothing.

Dragging my feet through the shockingly not shitty grass, I made my way up to the top of a little hill at the edge of Brian's property. I stood at the top and took my dick out. Soft white lights shone from the windows of the other trailers in the horseshoe. It was nice to know that there were neighbors even all the way out in nowhere and I pissed into the dirt, hard and heavy.

I wondered who was in the house, what they were doing in the light. I wondered if the lights were like stars. If they had taken years and years and years to get to me from another galaxy. The people and their lights slowly dying, sending rays of photons and stuff cutting through the night to find people and ask for help. Guidance from someone. After all, they were all alone. It's hard to make it through the night that way.

At first the idea made me sad, but then it didn't seem too awful. Nice, actually.

I don't know how long I was standing there, but when I finally went to put my shit away it was small and cold. I tucked the stupid thing away into its nest and zipped.

When I turned to go, another light caught my eye. A room in the back of Brian's trailer. Should have looked away. Feeling like a voyeur was exciting though, so I didn't.

Brian was sitting on the edge of his bed. His eyes were closed. Face contorted up, twisted like a leper getting a suck job good enough to rip the damn thing off. Mentally skimming, I tried to recall any girls that had been there that night. Kelly had been around. Grace hadn't come by had she? My stomach sank. Did we know any other women? Then I got my answer.

A head bobbed up into view. Blonde hair. Side-swept bangs. New. He wiped his mouth in a comically exaggerated way. They high fived.

"Huh," I said.

HORSES

Soft crying came to me through the bathroom door.

"I'm sorry, I... I shouldn't have called you," Grace said. "It's just my parents are gone, and I couldn't have told them anyway and-"

"You don't need to be sorry."

"Well, I am. I'm sorry. And silly. It's not even... the blood has mostly stopped now."

I knew well enough to not ask her to open the door. Knew that from my own mother.

I remembered Mom. Locked on the other side of the door, the water running to cover the sound of her weeping. The snow falling outside, silencing everything but her. Crying. Mom called it the seasonal sad. My therapist would probably have a different name for it.

"If it weren't for you, I would kill myself," my mom had said.

She'd stay in for hours, locked up. The faucet was never loud enough to cover the sounds.

"What's wrong?" I'd ask. I wanted to fix it.

"I don't know. Nothing. Nothing's wrong, it's just... nothing."

I didn't know then that there was no way to fix it. That you find a way to live with it or you don't.

Dad would come home, confused. At a loss, is how he'd put it. *I'm at a loss*. Even then, somehow, as a kid, I had a better grasp of the hungry maw that stood before her than he did. It wasn't his fault. He couldn't understand it. How the sickness swallows you whole.

I didn't know then that one day I would understand exactly what she was feeling.

"You're the reason I'm still alive," my mom had said.

Even then I knew that kids shouldn't be the reason for anything.

I learned how to make my own dinners. I learned how to get away with what I did by forging her signature. I learned how to tell my dad it wasn't that bad, that I was okay. I learned to not ask someone to open the door.

Grace would come out when she was ready.

How, I wondered, sitting there with Grace, did someone stop the same stories from repeating endlessly in their lives? How was I right back on the other side of the door?

How many times would I need to learn lessons in my life before they took? So far my batting average was dogshit.

Grace said something. Her voice was so muffled, I couldn't make it out.

"Turn the water off," I said.

"You can go," she said. "I really shouldn't have called, it's not as bad as I thought. The bleeding has stopped now, really."

"I won't come in, but I won't leave you. Is that okay?"

She didn't say anything.

Then, "I cut too deep this time. I don't know what made me do it. It just..."

The water came back on and for a while we listened to it together, flowing down the drain. Comforting.

"Have you ever read *The Sorrows of Young Werther?"* I asked.

The water ran on.

"In it, there's this guy, Werther. Young Werther, I guess. He hates himself. He doesn't know what to do with all this pain, you know? Clever title. But at one part, he thinks about doing something bad to himself. And I think it scares him and confuses him. So he thinks about these horses, these wild horses, that, when they get really crazy while they're running, like overcome, you know, they can't breathe. So they actually, they bite their own veins open to get oxygen into their blood. They open a vein so they can breathe again. Because they're just too passionate. Like, too overwhelmed by it all."

I heard her body lean against the other side of the door. The pressure of her slid down, pushing against the barrier, and came to a stop on the floor with a little thump. I swear I could feel the warmth of her.

I said, "What's something you hate?"

"Hmm," she blew a raspberry. Smacked her lips. Thinking. "I hate Tyler Case."

"Who the fuck is that?"

"He's this guy I was in IB classes with. I went up to French VII and so I spent the last semester taking Spanish I. And he was in there with me, and he used to make these horrible Mexican jokes. He's a pig."

"What did he say?"

"Hm... so one time we had to cook a traditional dish from a country in South America and he said, 'Can I just bring in a bowl of dirty water?'"

I didn't mean to, but I laughed. Tried to cover my mouth but it didn't work.

"You're an asshole sometimes," she said on the other side of the door.

She was being nice about it, but she was right. "I know. I'm sorry. That's fucked up."

I put my hand to the door and imagined her doing the same.

"What's something that you love?" I asked.

A long silence.

Finally, she said, "I think... I think I love you."

I said, "I love you too."

PHIL

WE DROVE AROUND AND drank PBRs out of a cooler. New and Brian and Me. The three of us talked shit. Threw the cans out the window. Cigarettes, too. We were way out there for a while, in the real quiet country dark and the smokes flew through the air behind us, kicking off bright red ashes like tiny little fireworks in the dead night.

I didn't pay attention to where New was driving, just that he was vaguely getting us closer to town. I didn't realize where we were until he pulled into Candlewood Estates, a suburb on a hill cut out for the wealthiest of Rocky Mount. There weren't many, but there were enough. The old money earned from Jim Crow; the new money that had moved into Rocky Mount to make the cash go that much further. No matter where they got it from or when, they stood out against everyone around them.

Brian pushed his face to the car window. Breathing fog onto the glass of a human aquarium. "I heard a dude who used to play for the Hornets stays up here."

New drove the Jeep quiet and focused, like he knew where he was going.

I asked, "How many cars do you have? Where'd this thing come from?"

New didn't answer. He pulled the Jeep up in front of a house at the end of a cul-de-sac. Dark windows. Cold inside. Newspapers littered the driveway.

New stubbed out his cigarette. "Let's go for a swim."

"It's cold," I said.

"Yeah, it's like a polar bear club thing."

"How ya know they got a pool?" Brian asked.

He just knew. The backyard had a pool. Brian stood on the periphery of the backyard and lit a cigarette, while New peered through the sliding glass door. I squatted at the edge of the pool and cleaved my fingers through the water. Its chill numbed my hand, inside and out. For a moment we were all silent, the world was silent, the light dance of the water the only sound. Feeling numb was good. I wanted to tip forward until I sank to the bottom of the pool and let the cold fill me. How beautiful that would be. Then the sliding door opened.

We both stared at New, smirking with a now gloved hand on the door. I looked at Brian. He looked at me. Cigarette hanging from his slack bottom lip.

"I got it open. Check it out. It's nice inside."

We tiptoed, skittish mice knowing the trap will snap but hungry for the cheese. It was nice inside.

"How do you know they're not home?"

"Because I drive around this graveyard of McMansions looking for houses where the lights are always off and mail's piling up because Todd and Linda are on vacation, and they didn't even try to hide it because they're so fucking rich and arrogant. They think they're untouchable. Let's touch them."

New stepped inside the house. Spread his arms to show the breadth of his new domain. "They don't even have an alarm. We'd be hearing sirens by now."

Brian said, "That's just fucking stupid."

"Arrogant."

Then Brian said, "This is fucked up, dude."

"Allan is in."

"Of course, he's in! He ain't got any self-control or shit, his brain's fuckin' scrambled eggs."

"Fuck you, man!" I hissed.

New grabbed him by the shoulders.

"Allan is cool. And you're cool too. We're all cool. Now do you have my back?"

Stepping inside, I felt sick and weird. I knew I was going to steal something. Not even money, necessarily, which I needed. Just *something*. I wanted to take it because it wasn't mine. I wanted to break something because someone else had it. I wanted to go through their things and imagine what they did with them.

I hated myself for that, but I didn't stop.

I made my way through the living room, just taking things in, so excited to be outside myself, to be somewhere I wasn't supposed to be. Inside another house, another life. The furniture was all leather and shit. I didn't know exactly what made furniture expensive, but it looked expensive. The word rococo came to mind, though it didn't mean anything to me. It felt rococo.

A bunch of pictures stood on the mantel in frames that had words like 'Family' and 'Good Times' and 'Forever' on them. In one of them, a guy past his middle-aged prime held a giant Maine Coon cat in his arms. The guy looked paunchy and caught off guard. He stared slack-jawed into the camera. The cat looked like it had just come from the groomers and was modeling for Cat Sports Illustrated. It glared at the camera.

"Holy fucking shit!" New snickered. "They picked that picture because the *cat* looks good in it!"

With one finger I lightly pushed the picture toward the edge of the mantle. It fell onto the bricks surrounding the fireplace and shattered.

New giggled but Brian glared at me like I was the biggest asshole in the world. Whatever, dude. I looked at the next photo in line. Mom with big blonde hair and khaki capris with the two kids all dressed up. Cat Dad wasn't in the picture.

Brian wanted an asshole? I gave him an asshole.

I pushed that photo too. It fell next to the other, smashing and sending glass fragments flying into the carpet.

New clapped me on the back. Brian shook his head and walked away. I felt awful.

We split up. New went upstairs. I moved into the basement.

It was even nicer than Dank's. Cat Dad had his little man cave. There was the foosball table, bigger and better than Dank's parents'. A big stand-up cabinet arcade game stood nearby. Guns mounted at the ready. On the side there was a woman in a black leather jacket with a machine gun. She was straddling the Aerosmith logo and lowering her sunglasses in a way that said, "Come on and fuck me."

In the back, through a heavy door. The music room. Classic rock posters hung in thick wooden frames on the walls, broken up by photos of Cat Dad. This time he was posing with rock stars. Here he was whatever he wanted to be. He was actually smiling in these pictures, and he had perfect teeth and better posture. Down in the basement, our guy was a solid 7 for the local competition of dads. I named him Phil. He stood next to Don Henley, the guy from ELO, Santana. He had his arm around Pat Benatar. I wondered if he'd popped a Cialis before the show. Wondered what would happen if I took a Cialis.

In the center of the collection hung something beautiful. An autographed photo of Chris Gaines. On any other day he would have just been regular old Garth Brooks, but on this night, with his shaggy black bangs and soul patch, his brooding bedroom eyes, he was the one and only Chris Gaines.

Phil had spent a fortune on meet and greets, but Chris was the crown jewel.

But Phil walked the walk, too. Or at least had the gear to do it. On the far wall hung a dozen guitars and basses. Acoustics, electrics. In the far-left corner one called to me. A Fender

Precision Bass, tobacco burst finish. Looked vintage, 70's. Dust dulled its shimmering surface. A beautiful work horse, ready to work, sitting in a graveyard. It would blow my rickety knockoff out of the water. There was no way he was playing it. And if he suddenly needed to slap out the jams, he had three more to choose from. I took it off the wall... Threw the strap over my shoulder, felt the easy weight pull on me...

I wanted to walk away with it, but I couldn't. It didn't feel right to take someone's instrument for some reason. Even from Phil. Chris Gaines though, Tre would love that. We hadn't talked in a while, and I felt like I owed him something nice. I put the bass back, slipped the photo of Chris off of the wall, and turned off the light.

In the kitchen I found Brian sitting on the marble counter, slouched over, eating a sleeve of Oreos. I showed him Chris and he shook his head.

Carrying it with me, I moved upstairs. New stood in the master bedroom. Pockets so stuffed with jewelry that gold and silver ropes overflowed from their ragged denim edges. Frozen in place, staring at a wall covered in even more family photos. Five smiling people. Phil, Mom, the two kids. Maybe he felt the same way I did. I waited to see if he would smash them, too. Took a while for him to realize I was standing there. He went red. Tried to brush it off. He held up a prescription bottle in one hand and gave it a shake.

"Look what I found." Grinning, then.

ACCIDENT

When I pulled up the gravel stretch to Brian's trailer I found this woman sitting out in the dark on the porch all by herself, shivering in a sleeveless orange blouse, rubbing her arms. Fall was a little ways off, but it wasn't cold yet. Still warm and humid.

When I got to the porch I avoided eye contact and tried to hurry by her, but she said, "Hey, can I get a smoke off you?"

I held out a pack of Newports I'd accidentally ganked from Tre's car.

She wrung her hands together, real apologetic. "Oh, do you have anything not menthol?"

"I knew you were gonna say that."

"Sorry, I just, no offense, it's just those have fiberglass in them."

I dug through my pockets until I found a smashed soft pack of Pall Malls with a couple left. I handed it to her with my Bic lighter with a monster truck design on it.

"That's fuckin' cool," she said around the cigarette hanging from her lips and tossed the lighter back.

It felt weird to bum someone a smoke and not hang out. I had to wait it out. I lit up.

"How do you know Brian?" I asked her.

"Oh, we, uh-" She snorted an awkward laugh. "I wouldn't say we dated, we just. I, well, we got together a few times. Just hooking up, for fun."

For fun. She didn't have to say anything else; she was tweaking. I got it.

"Brian's a sweetheart," I said.

"Gotta stay warm out here," she said.

I nodded, rocked back and forth on my heels. *Cooooooooooool.*

"You know who he's dating?" she asked me.

"Brian?" The two of them in that room together. New wiping his mouth. Laughing. "Nobody," I said.

She turned away from me a little bit, looked out over the yard, at the road through the trees. "He said to me he's seeing somebody and couldn't mess around with me, but then he wouldn't tell me who it was. Got all weird about it. Not like it matters. I don't have to do stuff I don't wanna do. We were just having fun, partying together.

You seeing anybody? Cute guy like you, you probably aren't single." She tried to make it sound casual. Just small talk. Not an invitation.

"I've got a girlfriend, actually. She's here tonight."

"Good for you two! Hope you're in love. That's important. The most important thing."

She flicked her ashes out onto the porch floor. Took a long drag. Looking out into the night, she talked. Not to me, but to the darkness. Her voice slurred a bit, tongue sounding lost, as if it was stumbling from one unexpected word to the next.

"You'd've met me a year ago, I was in love. Heck, I didn't even use to drink much of anything. Never even smoked. I was a teacher's assistant, they test for drugs, what not, but then the thing with the car happened. My legs are still messed up.

They gave me these little pills, so they stopped hurting but didn't tell me about them and... heck, I didn't ask."

She looked at me. "You're in love, that's good for you. That's what's most important."

"Yeah, definitely. I need to go in and say hi and all that. My girlfriend's in there," I added. "But later, if you need a ride or something outta here, we can take you with."

She shook her head in tight little jerks. She held up her flip phone, a burner. "I'll figure it out. I'm trying to get hold of my husband to get off his ass and come pick me up."

When I got in I saw Grace through the sliding doors, smoking and talking to Tre outside. I was surprised to see him. She must have invited him. I'd assumed he wouldn't come and hadn't tried. They laughed together about something. Getting along famously.

I reminded myself that they'd known each other longer than either had known me. I wondered what she thought about his music. She laughed at something he said, and I felt weird for a second. Then they noticed me and waved, and I chilled.

I could tell neither of them were going to be spending much time inside with the rest of the scumbags tonight. After a few hangouts Grace hadn't wanted much to do with New for some reason and Tre wasn't coming back from the front porch scene.

Somebody else I didn't recognize was laying on the sofa watching *Next*. A guy on the TV said, "Two and a half minutes. I made it long enough to get a pack of smokes, I'm good." The person on the couch snickered.

Chanting and rhythmic pounding was coming from the kitchen, and I followed it and found Mohammed sitting across the table from Kelly. A bunch of folks stood around them, pounding on the table. Kelly was running a tattoo gun along Mohammed's forearm. It took me a second to figure out what she was making. A four cornered Celtic knot in a janky circle. Pagan, I guessed. I watched from the doorway. Brian wasn't anywhere to be seen.

New appeared beside me and handed me a beer.

"You look truly shocked Allan, it's fucking hilarious. Hey, where'd Grace go? She's totally ignoring me, it sucks."

"She's outside. Where's Brian? It's his house."

"He's in his bedroom, being all pouty. Too many people over. Whatever. He's being a little piss baby. I wish Kelly would stop doodling on these rejects. I was hoping to bang her tonight." He put his arm around me. "Look at all these troglodytes. These sweating mongoloids. It's very cool to be us right now.

I didn't disagree.

Kelly finished the tattoo. She tossed the gun on the table, and everyone gathered around to take a look. I couldn't see through all the sweating bodies.

Kelly said, "Sorry it's kinda wavy, the table was shaking from all these pounding dickheads."

"I love it, Kel. It's perfect." Mohammed leaned over and kissed her on the top of her head.

New clapped me on the back. "I'm not a tattoo guy, but you should get one. Remember this night forever."

"I'm okay," I said.

SICK

THEY SAY DON'T DO the afternoon at a strip club, but I don't know. It's alright.

I called Tre but he didn't pick up, so I dragged New and Brian with me to Satin Curves on a quest to watch this pregnant chick I'd seen there a few months back that was pretty hot, but she'd gone away to greener pastures. Or she wasn't pregnant anymore and I couldn't recognize her.

Instead, I sat at the edge of a wooden box with a pole in the middle of it and a mirror in the back and looked up at this Hispanic girl, dancing in a neon mesh outfit that she would seductively molt to the beat of "My Humps."

On a TV hanging in the corner, Donald Trump stood in front of a wrestling ring and talked to a super veined-out Vince McMahon. Bulging eyes, red faces. Sweat pouring. Intensity.

Brian laughed, took a long pull from a tallboy, and said, "This dude's awesome, man. He's richer than a bitch but he still loves this shit. They're gonna get in the ring together one day. Gonna be sick."

New tried to pull Brian away for something. A smoke. Or something more. I didn't care that they were sucking each other off, I didn't even think they were gay, not that that would matter either. But I didn't like that New gave Brian more attention and I fucking hated that about myself. I didn't understand what was going on. Was I gay for New? That didn't seem right. Brian didn't budge. New left, looking hurt.

I didn't mean to stare at Brian for so long, but the Vicodin slowed my response time, and he caught me. He jacked his eyebrows up in a little "*What, asshole?*" kinda look.

"Hey baby," the woman said. I looked up and she was smiling at me from on high. I threw a few dollar bills onto the stage, then stepped away. The beer and Vics had me a little wobbly. Hadn't gotten my sea legs for the day. I leaned myself up against the black painted wall in the hallway leading to the bathroom. The place reeked of piss. I called Tre. The energy between the three of us was getting weird and I wanted a new element.

When he picked up I held the phone out so he could hear the sounds of the matinee show.

"Are you at a strip club?" he asked.

"Maybe. Wanna come?"

"Uh... I'll pass. I don't pay for that stuff.."

I didn't like his judgment, but I pushed it down. "We're not gonna be here all day. Wanna come hang out with me and the guys?"

"Sorry, I'm good. I got this Korg synthesizer from the 90's and it's like, surprisingly sweet. Kinda going down a rabbit hole here."

"Maybe some other time? You and me?" I sounded pathetic but I missed the guy. I hadn't seen much of him at the last party, and he'd ducked out early.

When I got back to the stage Brian was gone, New was back, and the stripper was sitting on the edge of the stage, checking out an open wound on her ankle. The Ying Yang Twins whispered from the speakers.

"Oh shit, what happened?"

New looked up from texting on his phone. "Huh? Oh, Brian left, he's being super weird about- Just, I dunno. He had to make a phone call or some shit."

"No, I mean to her, dumbass."

"There's a nail," she said, pointing at a nail sticking out of the edge of the stage.

I leaned over the wound. It wasn't long but it was surprisingly deep. Like a gouge, they might call it. She didn't pull away from me while I looked.

"Hold on, I got you." I turned to the bartender and asked did he have a first aid kit.

He didn't check. Instead, he pointed to a table where somebody had left a bar rag.

I hustled over and grabbed it. Moist. I came back and pressed it against the lady's ankle.

I said, "I think there's still cleaning stuff on it, like bleach or something, so you should be okay."

"You're cute," she said. "For real, not just for work."

"Thank you," I said.

Her tits were still out, and she cupped one, gave it a little jiggle for me. It was all getting too intimate too quickly. Patients always fell in love with their nurses. I held the rag to her ankle and stared at the ceiling, waiting for the bleeding to stop.

"What do you wanna do?" I asked New.

"I don't know. Nothing. I don't care." He slammed his phone shut and tossed it on the top of the stage.

"What's Brian wanna do? Like, is he over it here?"

"You and I can do whatever, Allan." New's face was scrunched up all tight and dark.

"Wanna go get piss drunk?"

He shrugged. "Sounds perfect."

"We gotta fix these nails," the lady said.

DELHOMME

Karaoke night at Gator's. Grace was in Raleigh with Kelly at a David Sedaris reading. Tre hadn't picked up the phone when I called. Brian and New had come in with me but were being all weird and had disappeared again. I sat at a high top with Mohammed nursing beers and sinking into a Xan bath.

A fat fuck sat at the end of the bar in a Delhomme jersey stretched to its absolute fucking breaking point. Fucking Delhomme. Our almost hero. Fat Fuck must have been a bit thinner in 2003.

In the corner, standing tall on the wooden platform, a middle-aged woman in a sweatshirt airbrushed with a Tweety Bird in a backwards Kangol was singing "I Can't Make You Love Me" with more conviction than I'd ever felt for anything in my life. On the edge of tears. My mom used to listen to that song when she'd had some red wine. I hated it.

I thought about getting hit by a car. How good it must feel to be obliterated into nothing. I resented Grace for being gone that night at the same time I knew that was fucked up. Wondered if the stripper I'd helped with her blood would come in. I could sweep her off her cut up ankles.

I don't know how long it had been since Mohammed and I had spoken when he suddenly said, "I think I accidentally took one of those sexual enhancement drugs with that Xan bar. I thought it was a Soma, but man... I think it was the opposite."

He laughed to himself. We watched the woman sing.

He said, "She's beautiful. Got the voice of an angel, but she is making me pretty hard right now and there is... there is no reason for that. I definitely messed up here, Al."

I finished my beer, grabbed my Baileys, and walked outside to the parking lot. I lit up and felt the chill of the night crawl over me. Across the parking lot, New and Brian were into something. I couldn't hear them, but New was running hot, hands gesturing all crazy and Brian was looking up and away, defiant and over it all.

I crept across the parking lot, holding close to where the floodlights bled into shadow. I worked my way around until I got to a rusted out pickup only about ten feet away from them and hid on the other side. I heard Brian first.

"I don't get why this is such a big ass deal to you, dawg."

"I just... I just want to hold your hand. Not like now. In front of people. They're our friends, they'll understand."

Brian laughed. It was bitter and cold, like ice cubes in his mouth.

"You don't get it. I'm not from Chapel Hill. Shit's different here."

I peeked my head over the hood of the truck. New moved toward Brian and tried to take his arm. Brian pulled away.

He said, "Look man, I like you. I do. You're fucking cool, but I think you're like misunderstanding what's going on here. I ain't a faggot."

"Can you say that with my dick in your mouth?"

"Man, fuck you."

"And by the way, I'm not gay either. I'm whatever I want to be."

"Okay," Brian said. Then, softer, "I'm sorry, Newton. I am. For real."

I watched Brian walk away and get in the truck. He pulled out, hitting New with his high beams, flickering him to life in the dark. Tears ran down his face. A tragic film reel, burning out frame by frame.

I stomped my smoke out and went inside before New caught me watching him. The lady was clearing her throat for a second song. No competitors tonight. I sat back down with Mohammed and tried to pretend I hadn't just seen what I'd seen. Mohammed slapped me on the back and ordered us another round of shots and beers. He smiled at me, big.

"What's wrong, you look down and out. You okay?" He gripped his crotch through dirty jeans. "I'm still rocking a little half chub thing here."

He leaned in close, his whiskey breath hot on my face. He whispered as if the lady could hear anything over her own rendition of "It's All Coming Back to Me Now."

"Her voice, it's beautiful. I realized something. That's what's getting me hard. I checked my pocket. I *did* take the Soma! It's just her passion that's taking me there. That's powerful."

Her voice was beautiful. And lonely. And vulnerable.

We listened to her, and I felt so alone, and I just wanted to go back to Goodwill and pretend to be somebody else again. Instead, Mo and I stayed and drank boiler makers for hours and watched our starlet sing until we were falling off our stools.

FIRE

IT STARTED WITH ME and Kelly and New. New was driving a fresh smelling Honda minivan. He had a cooler in the back and there was a case of thirty-six Tecate beers inside. We decided that we were going to drink them all. He drove fast. The night was cool and felt good rushing through the cab of the car. We threw cans and cigarettes out the window.

We drank a lot of beers and had to piss so we stopped on an old bridge. New and I pissed into the Tar River. Kelly pulled her ripped jeans down around her ankles, hopped up on the rail, hung her ass over the water. To keep her anchored, New grabbed one hand, I grabbed the other and she leaned back, pissing out into space. It went on forever, infinite, beautiful. It was dark but I saw her pussy for a second and she had an overgrown landing strip and I felt bad and turned on. I hoped she didn't notice.

Later we stopped at a gas station. I put gas into the van while New went in to buy some smokes. Under the phosphorescent light of the gas pumps Kelly pulled the shoulder of her shirt down to show me a square of white bandaging.

"Check this out!" She pulled the bandage back to reveal a little sparrow tattoo, flitting toward her collar bone. Done in the old school sailor throwback style that was getting popular.

New came back out with Marlboro Reds and a twelve pack in his hands. "This was all they had," he said.

"How'd you get beer?" Kelly asked.

"What do you mean?"

"You're not twenty-one," I said.

"Oh, yeah, well, I dunno. I just showed her my smile." And he flashed it at us.

Kelly thrust her shoulder toward him. "Check out my ink."

"I already saw it."

"I didn't put it on Myspace yet, where'd you see it?"

"On a thousand other people."

Her drunk grin soured. "You're a fucking dick, Newton. You should go home."

She marched to the back of the van and crawled inside. I laughed. New didn't.

"She's-a never gonna let me eat-a that ass-a now!" He said it like Mario and twirled an invisible mustache but kept a straight face.

"Sure," I said. "How'd you really get the beer?"

He shrugged. "Walked out with it."

He always got what he wanted. Like magic, New.

"I'll be right back," I said.

I walked into the store, wandered through the shoulder high aisles, trying to find a blind spot between the lady behind the counter with the fading-to-blue wedding ring tattooed on her finger and the really big guy in Carhartts she was talking to on the other side of the counter. I found a pack of peach rings and slipped them into my pocket. I walked real casual to the door.

"Didn't your mama ever tell you not to steal?" the woman asked.

I stopped, turned. I don't know what my face looked like, but they were both trying to not laugh. For a second I thought about running but the guy was really, really big. I put the candy back while they watched. The lady took my picture and told me I couldn't come back while blowing on the Polaroid. I went to the van empty-handed and embarrassed. Kelly was asleep in the back. New drove away without asking what happened.

We drove on, drinking and tossing. I said, "We should call Brian up, rip some rails. I feel like I could do this all night."

New kept his eyes on the road.

Later, I showed New where there was an open side entrance to my old high school. He pulled into the back, where I used to load in sets for the plays we did. Furniture and flats from the fall performance of *Tartuffe* slumped ragged and molding against the bricks. He took the twelve pack out and I climbed in the back and pushed Kelly over on her side in case she puked.

With the help of a dumpster, we climbed up on the roof. I dug a PBR out of the case and lit a Baileys.

New rubbed his eyes and blinked into the night. "Do you ever think you're a piece of shit?"

"Are you calling me a piece of shit?"

"No, I'm saying me. I feel like that. But have you felt like that too?"

I sucked the beer down like Eli Wallach in the desert and tossed the can off the ledge, not far from the backdoor. I imagined the face of my drama teacher, coming in and finding it there. I knew it would hurt him and I liked that. I opened another beer.

"Oh yeah. All the time. I saw a doctor about it once."

"Did it help?"

"No. I don't think anything will." I hoped that wasn't true. I flicked my cigarette into the open side of the dumpster. There was a bunch of cardboard in there. I lit another one.

New said, "I had a stepdad once who always said I was going to end up in prison. I told him it was better than having a room temperature IQ."

"You had a stepdad?"

"You ever think we're hopeless? I mean it. Do you think we're headed somewhere really bad?"

The beers were hitting him hard that night. Things were shifting into darkness. I didn't want to agree with him, but sitting there on that roof, nothing in front of me, nothing behind, I couldn't exactly disagree. I clinked my can against his.

"To somewhere really bad," I said.

"To somewhere really bad," he said.

About then the dumpster went up in flames. The first time you see a fire take over it is shocking. New smiled down at it. We jumped the fifteen feet onto an old prop sofa and bounced off onto the pavement.

New peeled out, taking that mini-van as hard and as fast as it would go. He left black marks on the road leading out of the school and gunned it down the state highway. Sleeping cows went by so fast. Blue and red lights lit up the road in front of us and he slowed just in time for the cops to crest the hill and come up on us. The sirens wailed like hell as they sped past.

In the back Kelly spoke up, slurring. "What the fuck is going on? What did you *foreskins* do now?" There was some affection in her voice.

Up front, we howled with laughter.

Here's to somewhere really bad.

GIG

TRE BUMMED ME A smoke and I lay back on the trunk of the LeBaron. The metal popped under my weight, leaving a perfect ass dent.

"Hey," Dank said as he slid his bass into the backseat.

"Hey."

He high fived me and walked back into the basement of the church.

"Good show tonight, man."

It was true. I'd showed up unannounced to watch the Jazz Disaster play and he'd seemed genuinely glad to see me. His smile was a relief.

"Thanks," Tre said. "Can't believe we played a church. They were cool with it because it's just instrumentals but if they knew what that synth was saying they'd be condemning me straight to hell."

He flicked his cigarette onto the pavement. Toed it out. He looked down as the embers smoldered, smoke rising. He stabbed another into his mouth and lit it.

"I've been meaning to tell you, actually..."

I sat up with a groan. "What's up?"

"You remember Art Lord and the Self-portraits? From Greensboro."

"Yeah."

"They hooked us up, got us signed to their label. It's small, but still. They already booked us studio time in Charlotte. We're gonna record an EP in like a month."

"...oh." I didn't know what to say. "That's awesome."

"Thanks, man. That means a lot."

"You ever need a bongo player or a harmonica guy or something, I'll totally practice those Joy Division songs." I felt embarrassed suddenly and changed the subject. "Oh hey, I got this thing for you."

I pulled out the Chris Gaines photo I'd had in my trunk for the last week. Tre took it and started laughing. Big, loud laughs that made me feel good.

"Where in the heck did you get this, man?"

"New and I broke into this dude's house up in Candlewood. I found it in this room he had, this music room, with all these photos in it and- What?"

Tre wasn't laughing anymore. He was staring at me, hard.

"Why do you do shit like this? You have options, man. You have so many choices. I just... I don't get it."

"I... What else am I supposed to be doing?"

He kept staring at me, but his eyes softened. He handed me the Chris Gaines photo. He spread his arms and leaned in toward me.

"Is this... are you hugging me?"

He wrapped them limply around me and pushed his thin chest against me. "You're a good guy. Be safe, okay? Hit me up if you wanna go fishing sometime."

I patted him on the back. "Yeah. See ya, Tre."

I drove way out into the night, into the country, and stopped on some old bridge. It wasn't until I got out and walked to the railing that I realized it was the same bridge we'd all pissed off of. I was moving in circles. I took the Chris Gaines photo and smashed it on the rusty metal railing. I whispered a prayer to him in the darkness. *As goes piss, so goes Chris. Sayonara, soul patch.*

I threw it over the side and watched him fall, fading into the darkness.

WASTED

After the parking lot fight at Gator's, Brian disappeared completely. I missed him. He chilled New out. Kept things from going too far when I couldn't. I'd tried to play therapist. Pretended I hadn't been spying and asked New what had happened between them. He didn't want to talk about it.

The other thing though, was the drugs. When Brian went, so did the pills. No more Oxy. No more Vics. No more Addies.

New didn't want to talk about it.

Without the drugs, a hole opened up in me. I sunk into someplace dark. Days just spread out in front of me. I hid in the house and didn't talk to anyone, even Grace. The world had lost color, kept only its rough edges. It wasn't like I was shaking and sweating, begging for pills. It was all in my head. But that didn't feel too much better.

Of course, it didn't occur to me how I'd gotten there. How just months before I'd met a guy in a Waffle House parking lot. How a doctor had given me a diagnosis I'd ignored.

Even though I hadn't been to class in weeks I decided to work on the Criminology 101 project to kill time. I hid in my bedroom, cutting out pictures of Ted Bundy and drinking. I'd stolen some cash from where my parents kept it in an old flour tin and bought a couple handles of Rebel Yell and I mixed it into my mom's little bottles of Diet Coke without arousing suspicion.

So I pissed away hours staring at the wall, smoking, doing the Bundy thing for the crime lady who stayed in Raleigh, desperately wishing that Brian would appear from thin air, his hands overflowing with pills, a halo of light around his head shimmering like a saint so I could gobble them gratefully down and get out of my head, get out of my life, get out of the crushing nothing that was all around me again.

I wouldn't have gotten out of bed that day if Grace hadn't shown up.

Mom took her to my room. (*"We've heard so much about you!"*) She hadn't. I had kept pretty much everything with Grace a secret. It made it more special, I guess. We had something that was just between the two of us. Us.

She sat on my bed with her Chucks on. That little black heart, broken in two. True. Love. She looked at me, sad wet eyes. I didn't want to look at them. They made me feel like I was a bad person in a way I couldn't explain. They gave me the feeling, somehow, that there was something awful looming on the horizon, something that I wouldn't be able to avoid because

I, too, am bad. She was trying to warn me, but even she didn't know it.

"Are you sick?" Cute little voice, like a cartoon bear would talk. "Do you want me to make you some chicken soup?"

I shook my head. "I'm not hungry. I don't want to eat."

"Are you, you know, feeling okay?

Your mom mentioned you're seeing a therapist? You didn't tell me that. It's good, right? Did she..."

Wrapping both of her hands around mine, tentative and delicate, a girl holding her sick dog, she trailed off.

I shrugged. I just wanted her to go away. I wanted to feel anything other than whatever my brain was doing. For a moment I thought about calling Brian but then I realized I didn't even have his number. He was gone now.

"Seriously. Are you okay?" she asked.

"Yeah," I said. "I'm fine."

"You don't... you don't seem fine."

I needed a drink. A Perc. A Vic. An Oxy. Morphine. Numbness. I wanted the sun to go out.

"You're sick. Depressed. When was the last time you hung out with Brian?" She was gentle but pushing.

"I dunno, Jesus. It's been a while, he disappeared."

"Do you think that maybe..." She rubbed her hands together like little paws. "Do you think you're like this from not getting high?"

"What the fuck?" Exposure. Anger hit me like I'd shot it into my vein. Red hot.

"I'm gonna go get a pickle from the kitchen." She got up to go.

I grabbed her by the wrist, harder than I meant to. "What do you mean by that?"

She wrenched her arm away from mine and sat down heavily on the edge of the bed, outside of my reach. She knew I wouldn't move to stop her again.

"You have a fucking problem, Allan."

Her head hung low, strands of bright red bleeding into dark brown roots hanging like a funeral shroud over her face. When she finally looked up, pushed the lace back, she was crying.

"I took the test twice. To be sure."

"Test? You- You already got into Sarah Lawrence." Really. I didn't get it.

She pulled her arms tight around herself. Hugging herself.

"Allan. I'm pregnant." It was a whisper.

Fuck. FUCK. I went back in my mind trying to figure out how this could have happened before I remembered that we'd been playing Russian roulette with our junk pretty much every single time.

"I pulled out though. Pretty much every time."

"Yeah... It doesn't really work like that." She wiped snot on the back of her hand.

"We weren't like... super responsible, huh?"

She shook her head. I opened the covers. She hesitated, then scooted over. Her head on my shoulder felt like the weight of everything, pinning me down. It also felt safe. Keeping me in place while it crushed me. I finally put my arm around her and held her tight.

"I know keeping it's not smart, but... I do dumb stuff all the time," she said.

"What jobs pay for a baby?"

"You like Taco Bell."

"I'm serious, man."

"I know, sorry. I'm uncomfortable so I'm making jokes."

I loved her even more then and I knew that this was gonna hurt bad no matter what.

"I could join the Air Force. They don't require a lot of discipline I don't think."

I tried to sound casual. I was terrified. I felt like I was going to vomit. I wondered if she could feel my hands sweating through her shirt. I pulled my hand away, then wondered if that would make her feel unloved, unsupported. I put my sweaty hand back.

"I'm supposed to go to school, but... I don't know. It's a part of us, together, or it could be, and..." she hesitated, choked something back. "And I love you. I don't want it to be gone."

"Just for it to not be there to start."

I thought of the little guy or girl curled up in there, in her belly, asleep. My parts and her parts all mixed together to make something new. It didn't ask for two idiots who couldn't wear a condom. I wondered if it could hear us.

Ending it would end us. The us I knew and liked. Hotel parties, fucking, drinking and loving and crying. Could any of it have gone on forever?

TED

I WAS CUTTING OUT a photo of Ted screaming in court (*TELL THE JURY THEY'RE WRONG!*) with some round-tip Fiskars scissors I'd found from my elementary days. Mom had written my initials on them. AKD. I looked up to find her standing in the doorway. She was staring at Ted, chewing on her bottom lip. She had a big plastic state lottery cup in her hand filled with something.

She hugged me and held me tighter than I remember her ever doing it.

"...what're you doing?" she asked.

"Working on school stuff. Like you wanted."

"You're actually going to class?"

"I dunno. Sometimes... Not really. But I'm supposed to work on this thing."

She stepped closer to the bed. She was tentative. She looked down at Ted screaming in the courthouse.

Then she said, "Ted Bundy tried to pick me up in a bar in Florida."

I put the scissors down. "What?"

I pushed some stuff aside on the bed. She sat down at the edge, a couple feet away from me.

"Oh yeah. I went to college down there. I had friends in Tallahassee, going to Florida State. I almost went home with him. He was... charming. That part of the story is true. He was sort of good looking too I guess, but not like the way people talk about him now. I looked in his eyes and there was just nothing in there. Just black eyes, darkness. Dead back there."

"Jesus, mom."

"A couple years after college, I was hanging out. Just floating. This was before I met Daddy. I had another friend who was walking back home from a bar one night, alone. She disappeared. Never saw her again." She read my face and answered it. "It wasn't him; he was already in jail. This was just... some other asshole. It used to happen a lot back then and people didn't... didn't find the guy. I think they thought it would force us to settle down, if we were scared. No more bars or walking home alone.

They think if you're scared you won't be wild. But it's usually the opposite."

She picked up one of the cutouts, held it close to her. A deep frown creased her face.

"Maybe people are raising better boys. Like you."

"I hope so. And I'm... I'm glad you didn't fuck Ted Bundy."

"Me too." She sighed. Took a breath. "You've been drinking a lot of those Diet Cokes. I'm gonna have to go up to the Food Lion today."

"Sorry. I'll go buy some. I'll uh, I'll walk down there later."

"Yeah, don't take the car."

"...okay."

I hadn't planned on saying anything to her. I didn't want to tell anyone.

"Mom, I... I think I need help. I've been partying a lot, getting fucked up. We're taking these like, painkillers and I, I dunno, I feel like I like them more than I should sometimes."

She cocked her head, confused. "So, what, you're like shooting up?"

"I'm... no. I mean, they're pills, you know?"

"Like Tylenol?"

"What? No. They're not like-"

"You said they're pills."

"It's different. They're phar- pharmac- they're pharmacy level."

She took a sip from her cup. "So, a doctor prescribed them to you? Is this that psychiatrist? Finally doing something, I guess."

"They weren't prescribed to me exactly..."

"But they're from a doctor, right? They're medicine."

I shrugged.

"I wouldn't worry about it. Don't be too hard on yourself. Okay?" She took a long drink and thought about something. "It's good to be hard on yourself, but sometimes I think you, Allan, you're either not hard enough or you're *too* hard. I think some of that's my fault, Allan. It's hard to be a mother. A parent in general, but a mother, that's... that's harder. No matter what people say, that's harder."

"Stop saying hard."

She reached out and took my hand and I jumped.

She said, "One day you'll want to kill yourself. Please promise me you won't."

I said, "What?"

"You didn't really know Pa, he died when you were six, but he... he wasn't great to your uncle and me. Every generation tries to do better than the last. It's all we can do. I tried my best, but... He gave something to me, and I think I gave it to you. I know you're gonna have this feeling inside you. Just promise me."

I nodded.

"I need to hear you say it. Promise me, sweetie."

I took a gulp from my Coke.

"I promise," I said.

FINGERED

NEW POPPED THE BLADE out of the box cutter. I winced just looking at it. It stared back at me, rusty and dull, ugly.

"How long since you used that thing? Looks like you've been carving figurines out of dog shit with it."

"Shut up. You don't care," New said, sharper than the blade.

"That is true."

I pulled my legs up under me, trying to get comfortable on the top of the hood of News' car, this time an old sedan. Somebody's car. I'd never seen it before, and I didn't know where New got it. Like the others, I didn't ask. The backseat was filled with dirty blankets and a bunch of socks wadded up in a t-shirt to make a pillow. Like he'd been living in there. I didn't ask about that either. I was more interested in what he had found: A single morphine pill. Apparently it had been in the inside pocket of an old denim jacket for who knows how long. He'd found it right on time. We were both about to crack open.

How long had it been? A week? We didn't know, but without big pharma time was becoming real again. The world was making itself known. We were becoming aware of our bodies.

The single white pill sat on top of a dusty DVD copy of *Freddy Got Fingered* that New had found under the back seat of somebody's car.

"Thanks for sharing," I said.

He shrugged. "It was this or do it alone."

I was surprised he hadn't picked alone.

New used the boxcutter to cut the morphine in half. Delicate, reverential, respectful as a prayer. We were talking to God. Snap. It parted cleanly, leaving a few medicinal grains spread over Tom Green's orgasmic clown face.

I picked up one end, New took the other. We swallowed them dry. No crushing up lines. No parachuting for pleasure. Those were old rituals from a different time.

Before I could ask, he'd licked his fingertip and collected the leftover crumbs. Rubbed them into his grinning gums.

"Can we watch *Freddy Got Fingered* later? I like the part with the baby and the uh, um, the uh, paralyzed girl."

"Fuck. Yeah." He cracked open the DVD case. Empty. He tossed the box out into the field. It disappeared into some tall grass.

I scrolled through New's iPod, connected from a six-foot-long cable into a cassette in his cassette deck that would play whatever you plugged into it. A magical tool. The cable was just long enough to sit out on the hood with it. I clicked on Pig Destroyer, *Terrifyer*, and a nightmare spilled out of the car's open windows. It was bone crushing and I liked the way its weight overcame me, the way the blast beats vibrated through the hot metal and up into my ass made me feel like I had to take a nice, warm shit. It was a hug from a monster.

New coughed out a choked laugh, strange and cold. He said, "I love that you wanna listen to this man, but I can't handle it. I'm going dark already, I need something like, sweet."

He had *I'm Wide Awake, It's Morning*. I hated Conor Oberst for actually making something I loved, but I couldn't deny it. I scrolled down to "Lua" and clicked. That trembling voice, threatening to catch and fall into tears. New nodded along. I had picked well.

We laid there until the song was over and it moved onto more sad strumming.

Then New said, "I know you think Brian is a nice guy, but he's not."

I couldn't tell him what I'd heard that night. What I knew. It would kill him to be so vulnerable and exposed.

"Okay, well, I like him. He's gone anyway, right?"

"I know him better than you do, and I can't explain to you why, but he's not."

"Okay," I said, hoping he'd leave it alone.

"He's leaving town in a few days. He'll be gone for a week. That trailer will be empty except for all the money and pills that he keeps there."

"*And Days of Whore.*"

He sat up and stared at me, opioid pin pupils stabbing into me. He looked possessed. Maybe he was.

"I'm serious," he said. "All those dream seeds are being used by a bad person."

I didn't meet his eyes. Didn't even sit up. I just lay there on the hood, head propped up on the windshield, looking out over the field in front of us. I was scared. I said, "He shared a lot of that stuff with us."

"Yeah, to get us hooked and cut us off so we'd have to buy it from him later. He's a fucking drug dealer, Allan. He's a scumbag."

"I'm not hooked. I'm not like, a sick junkie. We're just hanging out."

"In four days, I'm gonna break into his shithole trailer and steal everything I can. I can do it alone or you can come and help me and have half of it."

My face felt numb. I sat up and rubbed it, trying to massage blood into my brain, trying to give myself some clarity of thought and wishing to hell that New hadn't waited until the morphine was kicking in to talk about this. "He'll know it's us. We've literally done a burglary with him already."

"People get robbed here all the time. Do you have any idea what the crime rate is in your town? I read the news, you should too. And *everybody* knows he's basically a pharmacy, he's a prime candidate for robbery. Besides, Brian's not the smartest fellow in the world. He's actually kind of dumb. Like somewhere between cheesy bread and plankton."

"I think he just has an accent, man."

"Whatever. He won't even be home, so there's that."

"What if neighbors see us?"

"We'll wear masks, we'll put on different clothes. We'll go to Goodwill, it'll be fun."

"The money too?" I asked.

"Of course, the money too. I will not fuck you over. We're friends, man. I'm sticking with you. Till the bitter end."

"I'm sorry, man, I... I don't know. Can we go somewhere?"

We parked in the church parking lot across the street from Gator's. I'd wanted to grab a beer and think about it, but we'd spotted Tre and Grace sitting on the curb out front. Something about it felt weird. We pulled over to watch them.

This fat Black lady was sitting behind the wheel of a Cadillac a few spots away. She was eyeballing us hard. Sizing us up. I couldn't blame her. Two White scumbags, pupils in little morphine pinpoints. Suspicious as hell.

They sat together, thigh to thigh on the concrete. Locked in some deep conversation that seemed difficult one moment, funny the next. They were fidgeting and flirty. They looked deep into each other's eyes, nodding along. He playfully shoved her with his shoulder. She put her calf over his and nestled her shoe into his inseam.

I punched the dashboard until my knuckles were raw. New let me work it out.

He said, "I need you, Allan. Are you in or out?"

New needed me. And so that was that.

“Okay,” I said. “I got your back.”

GUN

Back by the river again.

Tre was the last person I wanted to see, but I needed to confront him before whatever happened at Brian's happened. I hoped I had what it took to kick his ass. That I wouldn't choke on friendship.

I was grateful to him for one thing: he'd brought a thermos he'd mixed up a batch of bloody marys in. They were spicy and heavy with liquor. And getting warmer with every minute we spent sitting out there.

Tre stood by the water. He had his pole in his hand, but his line wasn't in. It hung in the air, a little rubber squid thing dangling off of it, glittering in the sun.

I wanted to run up and push him in. Hold his head down until the bubbles stopped. He still had no idea that I'd seen him with Grace though, so it would have been kind of pointless without a big preamble.

"Just watching a river... Man. We should go golfing sometime. You have to find stuff to do while getting fucked up. That's what makes it fun."

I lifted my head just enough to give him an arched eyebrow.

"Getting fucked up is doing stuff."

He shrugged and turned back to the river.

The water ran on and on, cutting through the earth and carrying all kinds of debris to places far away.

What will you remember when you go?

I had a vision of us when we were kids. Before New and Grace and pills.

We were Huck and Finn. Two country urchins hammering together a boat and lighting out on some adventure. Sailing the high seas in search of cold beer and warm pussy. A journey that would take both of us far away from whatever our future selves had gotten into and whatever dumb shit we might have kept doing to carve a place out in Rocky Mount, North Carolina. If you don't leave you have to succumb. You don't buy a gun with the numbers scratched off for no reason.

The gun.

The gun would help at Brian's, I thought. Just in case there was a hero neighbor or something. To scare them. I wouldn't load it. It would just be a precautionary thing. A tool. Like a hammer. Something to ward away the evil in case someone came at us. Everybody stops when they see a gun. It could save our asses in the end.

"Hey, you know that gun you have?"

He slowly turned back to me. "...yeah."

"I'm going shooting with my dad and I was wondering, you think I could borrow it?"

"You wanna borrow a strap I bought off Zion to go to a shooting range with your dad?"

"Yeah. Why? Is that weird?"

Asking if something is weird means that yes, it is weird.

He kicked the dirt a little bit, leaned his fishing pole against a bush. It sank in, lost in the leaves. He groaned, then said, "It doesn't have anything to do with New does it? He and Brian are... You know that guy from the parking lot? He does the real thing, man. They're playing at it. Trailer trash shit. White boy shit."

"If you actually hung out you'd see they're good people," I said bitterly.

He laughed, hard and cold. "I saw enough man, I'm good. They're not good. Not for you, anyway."

I felt sick. I took a drink and let the warm tomato juice pool and sit in my mouth. I felt sicker.

"I don't need your advice, man. Save that for Grace."

He stiffened. Kept his eyes on the river. "Whatever they're asking you to do, just stay out of it. There's other ways to do pretty much anything."

"So..."

"So no, you can't borrow my gun to go to the shooting range. People don't need to be seeing that thing out in real life."

"Okay, that's fair," I said, trying to hold down how annoyed I was. Sure, he was right that it was trailer trash shit, but he didn't know that, and it pissed me off that he was making shitty assumptions about me and more pissed off that he was right. "You got any beer in the van?"

"Yeah, there's a cooler in the back with a few in there. Should still be kinda cold from last night. Grab me one, too."

I walked back to the road running along the river and followed its paved edge back about thirty yards to where the van was sitting in the grass. I went into the back first and checked the cooler. He was right. There were five Coors Lights and they were kinda cold. Check.

I dug through the shit sitting around in the cabin space looking for anything that might be heavy and metal and roughly the shape of a gun. I found an old roadside emergency bag and came up with this weird, dirty hammer-like thing that I think was supposed to be used to break the glass if you drive into water or something. In case of emergency. Not exactly gun-shaped, but it would do. I slipped it into my pocket, pulled two kinda cold Coors out of the cooler, hopped out of the van and peaked around the door. Tre was still standing at the edge of the water, looking out, lost in a dream that was far away from here.

I snuck around the van to the driver's side door and, trying to keep an eye on Tre, edged it open. It creaked louder than I expected and I froze for a second. I lost sight of Tre as I bent over and rummaged under the seat, running my hands blindly over the floor of the car. Looking... looking... I couldn't find it.

On impulse, I reached up to the bottom of the seat itself and there it was, wrapped in the old towel, secured under the seat by being jammed under the springs.

The gun.

A car went by, and I froze. They kept on. I popped my head up over the car hood. There was Tre, now fishing, line in the water.

I pulled it out, unwrapping it as fast as I could, shoving the pistol into the back waistband of my girl jeans. Tight pants were helpful. I wrapped the weird hammer up in the towel. He wouldn't see it, but he might feel it. I tucked it back up under the seat.

I stood back up and tried to look normal, glanced back at Tre. The pole stood in the ground, pressed into the soft dirt. He wasn't there. *Fuck.*

He wasn't behind me. I hurried around the van, a beer in each hand. I almost bumped into him rounding the van.

"Where you been?"

"Sorry, I was answering a text." I tossed him a beer. Real casual like.

"Texts. That's so weak. Come on man, they're starting to bite I think."

"Oh shit, let's go." I cracked my beer open and followed him back to the water.

Passing by my folding chair, I saw my cell phone sitting in the seat. I pushed past Tre and dropped down into the chair, covering it up before he could see.

"Jesus Christ," he said.

I shrugged. "Gotta sit, you gotta sit." I gulped at the beer.

Tre posted up by the water. He nestled the beer down into the mud and hauled the rod back as far as he could and whipped it, casting his line way out.

I slid the pistol out of my waistband and dropped it into my backpack. I wandered over to the river's edge and stood next to Tre. We watched the bobber float upon the water, moving gently with the river.

"I saw you and Grace. At Gator's."

His shoulders slumped. The rod sagged in his hands. "We were just talking."

"It was all flirty and shit. I saw it. Like, giggling."

I'd been fantasizing about killing him but now I couldn't even look at him. My voice stayed low, controlled. He was still my friend.

"She was worried about you. I was, *am*, too. You're fucked up. You don't see it? We were talking about you. It was an intense conversation. We've been friends forever; I've known her longer than you have. I was trying to keep things light."

"She's fucking pregnant," I said.

He didn't say anything to that. I pushed on.

"Still wanna fuck her now?"

"We don't wanna do that."

"She did the foot thing, that thing where she puts her Chuck against yours and-"

He stabbed the end of the fishing rod into the dirt. He turned to look at me. I turned to look at him. Our eyes locked in like theirs had.

"Okay, fine, maybe I did, in just that moment, wanna fuck her a little bit. Maybe she wanted that too, I don't know. I'm so sorry that I wanted to do that for even a second, and I'm sorry you saw it man, that's fucked up and I get it. But it doesn't matter, because she loves *you*. I do too. So fucking much, dude. I don't know how you don't see it. I don't know how you don't know in your bones that even if we wanted to we would *never* do that. We couldn't. Our souls wouldn't let us. If you don't understand what I mean by that then I'm sorry because I don't know how else to say it.

Are we cool?"

"Yeah," I said. "We're cool."

I knew in my heart that he was right, but I felt like a pussy for not trying to kick his ass. I decided to keep the gun.

Then we drank beer and watched the bobber go up and down, up and down. It knew to do exactly what it was supposed to. It jerked under water. Once, twice. It disappeared under the surface. Tre yanked on the rod and the line yanked back. He pulled again and then rolled back on the reel, pulling the line in.

"We got one!"

"Yeah. We got one."

Later I watched him cut the catfish's throat on a nearby rock. Its blood spilled out into the dirt. Tre stepped back and smiled at his catch. He wiped the blood off on his pants, leaving a little red stain, and folded up the knife. He mopped the sweat off of his forehead with the sleeve of his flannel and looked at me.

"Anybody ever told you not to do something because you're White?" he asked.

"I don't know..." I was embarrassed. "Rapping, I guess."

"Huh." He considered this. He picked up a pebble and tossed it into the water. Watched the ripples circle out until everything was still. "Yeah, I hate White rappers."

KO

EMINEM BLASTED OUT OF the open windows as we drove down the road toward Brian's empty trailer. New said that it made him feel fucking pumped up.

I already regretted taking the gun. There was no reason to bring it. Just an excuse for a cop to shoot us.

True to New's word. We'd stopped at Goodwill earlier in the day and picked up new clothes. My sweatshirt said I Hate Mondays. Garfield was falling asleep in his cup of coffee. New'd found a Cradle of Filth windbreaker that was actually pretty sweet. All paid for in cash.

My name was Brett Fox. His was Mickey Blue. Tonight, we were both outlaws.

He pulled over to the side of the road, into the grass and behind a large outcropping of scrubby bushes.

He pointed up the road a ways. "It's about 100 yards up that way."

"That's far."

"Jesus Christ, Allan. We can't just pull up to the front of the house, people will see the car. It's nothing. We're going to cut to the right, through those trees and then we'll basically be at his place."

I yanked our masks out from my backpack, letting the bag slump open at my feet. That's when New saw the gun.

"Oh, yes. I knew there was a reason I brought you into this."

Before I could shut the bag he had reached inside and come back with the 1911 gripped tight in his fist. The sight of it made something sick and evil and all-consuming come to light in my belly.

"I actually, uh, I don't think we need that. I mean, he won't even be home, so it's like- I stole it from Tre. I was drunk, it's stupid."

"It feels so... *real* in my hand." He looked at himself in the visor mirror and grinned at himself. "Every good outlaw carries a gun, Allan. We are definitely taking this."

"Yeah, I'd thought the same thing," I said. "Leave the clip out though?"

New hesitated, sighed, then released the clip and stood it in the cup holder next to a half-filled bottle of Mountain Dew Livewire with cigarette butts floating in it. Great minds.

"You don't need to be so worried. It's not like we haven't done this before. Calm your nerves, my friend. Take a deep breath."

I took a deep breath. I double checked that the clip was still in the cupholder before we got out.

When we emerged out of the tree line shrouding Brian's trailer from the road, the distance between us and his place seemed impossible. The trailer stood dark and even though it was a dumpy little thing, looked imposing as hell. The rest of the neighbor's mobile homes looked dead too. Slouching carcasses in an elephant's graveyard. None of them looked like they had anything worth taking. But here we were.

Our faces disappeared behind the ski masks. Two eyes behind a slit, nothing more. New's voice came out muffled and alien.

"What?"

Pulled the mask up. "These are dumb." Spit in the dirt.

I shrugged but left it on. *You never know.*

We made it across the property without waking anyone up and crept up to the door. Locked, of course. Smart move. New slipped a Harris Teeter rewards card from his back pocket and slid it between the door and the jamb. Twisted and pulled and we were there.

He moved in, quietly, confidently melding easily into the shadows of the dark trailer. He was gone.

Alone on the porch, I wished I was at the Harris Teeter eating the free cookies next to the cut out of the dragon with the pinwheel hat. I wished I was anywhere else.

I followed New inside.

The place was more fucked up than normal. Fast food trash and beer cans everywhere. Blankets and clothes laying around in piles. The scattered life of someone going through some shit. Poor Brian. New was already rummaging around. He pulled a drawer open to find a very thorough collection of Jean Claude Van Damme VHS tapes that we had no idea about. He snorted a laugh and left the drawer open.

Waving, I got his attention and pointed down the hallway. A soldier silently planning his next move with his platoon.

New pulled the mask up, revealing his mouth. "Just talk, dumbass. There's nobody here."

Then one of the blanket piles came to life, shifting and growing up from the couch until it was Mohammed, squinting into the dark. Disoriented, still drunk, startled, battle-hard Mohammed.

"Who the fuck are you?" he yelled. "Bri! Bri! Yo, Brian!" he yelled and yelled.

New yanked the mask down and slipped the gun from his waistband. Mohammed was on him, but he was fucked up and swinging wild. The butt of the gun came down on Mohammed's head. He fell back in a heap on the sofa. Blood ran down his face from a cut on his forehead. One arm rose in the air, locked stiff, and jerked in a weird way. A throaty, gurgling sound choked out of his throat.

Panicked eyes found me from behind New's mask. I moved toward Mohammed, wanting to help but not knowing how.

That's when the door in the hallway flew open. Brian stood in the doorway, wearing nothing but a Brooks & Dunn t-shirt, his dick illuminated by moonlight cutting through broken venetian blinds. It's strange the snapshots that stick in your memory. The things your brain decides to keep from trauma.

He saw Mohammed spasming and bleeding. Two masked men standing there, frozen like deer. The gun in New's hand.

The double-barreled shotgun must have been leaning just next to the door on the other side because it was in Brian's hands in a second. It was lighting up the room a second later. Closest to the door, I was lucky. I crouched by the doorway, hiding behind the Van Damme library. New, in the center of the room, had nowhere to go. Still, the first shot missed.

The second one didn't. Brian moved down the hallway like the Muscles from Brussels himself, blowing out the second barrel on New.

Pellets flew wide, but still caught him in the left shoulder and chest. They dropped him to his knees. The gun skittered across the floor and came to a stop near me.

Pride or instinct made him struggle to stay upright. The mask had never found proper purchase again and was riding up, exposing his neck. Three small holes pierced his throat, one dead center. Blood poured in urgent rivulets down his neck. He tried to say something to Brian but only gurgled.

The horror of it stopped Brian in his steps. He lowered the gun a bit and took the scene in.

New slumped to the floor, but somehow kept trying to push himself up with one elbow, his head slumping this way and that before jerking upright against the odds. A drunk trying to stay awake against the deafening wave of the black out. A fighter, desperate to shake off the KO pressing in on his tunneling vision, to not give in to the onslaught of fists, to go out, if he must, on his feet.

I wish there had been that moment where we locked eyes and he said, silently, *go*. Instead, his blood poured out in an impossible river onto the dirty carpet.

I grabbed the pistol off of the floor and burst through the sagging screen door. The door frame flapped shut against the vinyl siding, the rusty hinges crying out after me.

I ran as hard and fast as I could, until I hit the tree line near the road. Alone, I pulled my mask off and vomited in the dark. I looked back at the house, waiting, hoping for New to come out. Knowing he wouldn't. Just yellow light spilling out of the open doorway. That must have been when the mask came off. Brian's anguished howl cut through the night. It echoed in the trees. I knew then for sure. New wasn't coming out of there, ever.

I ran across the road and into neighboring farmland, cutting through the soft earth of a dead tobacco field. I stuck to the woods, moving along the direction of a state road that I was pretty sure would bring me closer to home. I dropped anything that might identify me as I went along, tossing it all as far away as I could, watching it land into the underbrush. First the mask. Then one glove, and the other. I wrapped the gun up in the sweatshirt and buried it in front of a pine I thought I could remember. Feeling naked, then. Shivering against the frosty night.

When the sirens rang out I was already a couple miles away. Just a young man out on a pleasant nighttime walk through the woods, underdressed and alone, tears streaming down his face.

SORRY

TWO DAYS LATER I knocked on Tre's grandmother's door and waited. The first days of fall were turning the world around me red, yellow, orange.

I was only wearing a t-shirt and the chill air was starting to sink into me. I clutched the package tight to my chest. The piece of metal wrapped in newspaper.

The door opened and Tre peered out at me through the screen door. I pulled the paper back to show him his gun.

He stepped back into the dark of the house and for a moment I lost him. I spoke through the mesh, into the shadows.

"I took it. I didn't shoot it, though. But I took it."

He didn't say anything.

I said, "I'm sorry."

He stepped back into the sunlight. His face was a twisted mess. Anger. Disappointment.

"I don't know who you are right now. Give it back right now and get the fuck out of here. This is the most fucked up-"

He stopped when he saw that I was crying. He might have realized it was happening before I did.

The door hit me, lightly, when he walked out onto the porch. He looked up and down the dying street. He pulled the gun from my hands and slipped it into his belt.

He hugged me. I started to wail. The tears came hot down my face. I couldn't stop.

We stood there on his grandmother's porch for a long time.

FAYETTENAM

What do you wear when a friend has been murdered?

It would have been an important question to New. Do it right. I settled on black skinny jeans, studded belt fitted to the side, black long sleeve shirt, black tuxedo jacket. The black Converses. Never die.

Kelly and Grace picked me up. They'd gone a similar way. Black dresses, torn black stockings. Goth sexy. New would have loved them. Grace had dyed her red hair jet black. She'd brought a liter bottle of Aristocrat Vodka that we mixed with some NOS energy drink. I had a bottle of Blue Raspberry Mad Dog 20/20 that I'd gotten a hold of somewhere. It went into the old bottomless purse with the razor blades and peroxide and hair dye and pregnancy tests.

Someone had talked the incredibly patient owners of Mucho Mexico Sizzlin' into letting us use the back room as a memorial space. Nobody had done anything to pretty the place up though. Folding chairs lined up in rows, a dozen or so in all. A picture of New stood at the front, a selfie from his Myspace page. His hair, streaked with blue, was kind of embarrassing. The photo had been blown up on a posterboard, making the resolution even shittier. It leaned precariously against an inflatable promotional bottle of Dos Equis.

In the daylight, the stains of the carpet and the bare walls and smudged windows were pretty bleak. I couldn't think of a more depressing place to be remembered. It was kinda funny and I thought New would have liked it in a way.

Grace drank heavy from the NOS bottle, and I didn't say anything.

Kelly cried a little bit. "The last time I saw him I called him a dick or something," she whispered.

"He was a dick, Kel." I patted her on the shoulder. "But he was fun."

Grace nodded at me and handed me the Mad Dog from her bag. She was hogging the vodka. How much did it take to get fetal alcohol syndrome? I didn't say anything.

A few other kids hung out, drinking from buckets of Dos Equis, and eating nacho trays that had apparently been part of the deal in getting the space from the restaurant.

Kelly got up and told a rambling story about how fun New was, how he had once traded her an Adderall for a random pill that she found under her car seat 'cause he was just cool like that, how he had held her hair back while she was puking in this very parking lot 'cause he was just a gentleman like that, how his death was proof that life was precious and beautiful and over so fast you guys, we need to all be so grateful for what we've been given and live in the moment.

It was actually really nice.

Some rednecky looking kids came in in the middle of her speech but they didn't interrupt. She ran out of steam anyway.

"Who's that?" I whispered, pointing.

Grace, already drunk, swatted my finger down. *Rude.* She squint-stared at them instead. "I don't know... Friends from back home, I guess? I posted about this on LiveJournal, so..."

After more speeches, the two groups slowly circled each other until we quietly mingled. I sidled up to a big ol' beefy boy in a Carhartt jacket and a ballcap cap with a fishhook on the brim. We are fishers of men. I handed him the Mad Dog and he drank hard.

"Thanks bro," he said and passed the bottle.

I took a drink. "You guys must be from Chapel Hill then, huh?"

"Naw, man," he twisted up, confused. "We're from the homestead. Fayettenam."

Fayetteville, or Fayettenam as we called it, vied for the title of shittiest, most ready to knife you in a parking lot town in North Carolina, going toe to toe with only Rock City. New was from Fayettenam. He'd left one void for another. Reinvented himself as the side-swept banged devil-may-care badass from the intellectual, indie, university town holy land of Chapel Hill. It had been a lie. It didn't matter now.

"Right, right. Fayetteville. I forgot. Glad to have you." I handed him the Mad Dog back and he accepted.

"Boot Scootin' Boogie" blasted out of a boombox. The new arrivals laughed, clapped, let out little whoops.

"What the fuck is this?" I asked my new Fayetteville buddy.

On guard now. He stood taller. "It's Brooks & Dunn." Defensive. "He loved this song, man. I mean it was kinda funny 'cause it's corny, but it was his mom's favorite song before she died," he said, soft and sad.

"I'm gonna go burn one," I said.

"You can smoke inside."

I stepped out. Lit a Baileys and sat on the curb. The late afternoon sun lowered behind fall trees, their branches already shedding to their skeletal frame in obedience to the coming cold.

Did I know New? Did they? I wasn't sure whether he was good or bad. In the night, getting fucked up, in the exhilaration of making trouble for no reason other than the sake of it, it didn't matter. Until he was dead, I hadn't really cared if he was a good person, just a good hang.

Why had Brian been home that night? Why was Mohammed there? A hangover, a flat tire, a late shift at work. Anything. I didn't care then, and I don't speculate now. Staying home was just one of the tiny, everyday choices in life that result in a person's death.

Like deciding to steal from your friend. Deciding to take another pill knowing it might drop you. Deciding to lie on the hood of a car in a parking lot and wait for life to happen to you.

Sitting there, I didn’t feel much more alive than New, whoever he was deep down.

Maybe it wasn’t too late. Maybe I could get some therapy.

I saw his shoes first. Brand new black Chucks for the occasion. Tre sat down on the curb next to me.

“How you holding up, man?”

I shrugged, stared at the pavement.

“I’m not gonna ask if the thing you returned to me had anything to do with why we’re here.”

“I swear I didn't shoot it.”

“I believe you.”

We sat in silence.

“So Dank wants to move over to guitar. The bass slot is open. We gotta start recording in a week. So. Get it together if you want it.”

He patted me on the shoulder. He got up and left. I stayed there on the curb until the sun went down.

NEED

I SAT IN THE car across from Brian's trailer, clear on the other side of the road, and watched through the tree line as the broken police tape danced like ribbons from the rails on the old wooden steps out front. I didn't see any activity, but I heard a lawnmower a ways off. Could be coming from the back of the property.

"What are we doing out here? I don't like it here," Grace said.

"I got something I need to do."

She looked at me, uncomfortable. Knowing.

"No, nothing like that."

I pulled my wallet out and left it on the dashboard. A little heavy handed, but she'd know I wasn't there to try and spend money.

"Well, whatever it is if you're gonna do it, can you do it soon? I'm hungry."

I didn't mean to, but I looked at her stomach and she covered it up with her arms, self-conscious. That was as good an exit cue as any. Whatever Brian was going to give me, it would be worse to stay in the car now.

I got out. Closed the door gently. Moving toward the trailer in the daylight felt different. When my feet touched the asphalt road, my knees almost buckled. The memory of that night came back to me all at once. I could feel the suffocating mask on my face and the adrenaline pumping through my veins.

Deep breaths. I pushed through and crossed the road. I forced myself to put one foot in front of the other and moved around the trailer to find Brian riding a mower deep at the back end of the property, close to some dense woods.

He didn't see me coming until I was already a few feet away from him. He was slumped in the seat and barely seemed to be paying attention to where he was moving the mower. He turned to look at me. Pinpoint pupils, sweating like crazy in the cool of fall. Beers sat in two cup holders on either side of him. They were both open. He looked away and didn't stop mowing.

"Brian," I said. Then again, louder, "Brian."

He stopped the mower. Turned.

"What?" He asked, his voice slurring even on that.

"I heard what happened. With New."

"Oh yeah? You heard?"

"Yeah... I uh, I wanted to know if you needed anything. Like if you need help or anything."

"Wasn't just New. There were a couple guys there..."

"I heard that too," I said.

He slapped at a mosquito on his arm but was about five seconds behind and only left a bright red handprint on his sunburned forearm.

"...three in all, I think." Finishing his thought. "I didn't think New had a lotta boys. Just us."

"Well, I didn't think he'd try to rob you either. People surprise you."

"True 'nough."

"How's Mohammed doing? I heard he got decked or something."

Brian picked up one of the beers out of the cupholder, realized it was empty, and tossed it into the grass. "He's good. Getting out of the hospital in a couple days. He'll be good."

"Good. I just wanted to see if you needed anything. And to say that I was really sorry to hear what happened. As your friend."

"Friend..." he echoed thickly.

"Maybe I could come by, mow your lawn for you. Though you seem to be doing okay with that yourself." I forced a laugh. He didn't. It looked like he'd been covering the same thirty square feet in a fucked up oval for the last day or so.

"Thanks, but I don't need nothing from you. So, you can, you can get on."

"Okay," I said.

I turned and walked away through the tall grass, quickly, looking over my shoulder as often as I could without being too obvious. He didn't turn the mower back on, but he didn't stare after me either. Just looked out at the horizon, like something was looming out there, waiting for him.

Back in the car, Grace smiled at me. It was nice to feel human warmth. It was nice to be with her. I felt lucky and disgusting at the same time.

"Everything go okay?" she asked.

"Sure," I said. "Let's go get some Taco Bell."

She pumped her fist in excitement as I pulled out, kicking up gravel.

CHANGE

FROM THE ROOF OF Grace's parent's house, you couldn't see much. A strip mall. A Chinese restaurant that had closed down. Roads. Paved veins cutting through the earth, taking people away from here. Away to where people played music or talked to therapists or got high or fell in love or listened to Brooks & Dunn with their mom. All beaming their lights out into oblivion, hoping that someone strong might see, might show up and help.

"How do you feel?" she asked.

"I'm not sure, honestly. We knew him so briefly, it's... this whole thing was so quick. It was like no time at all. But it was so long. I wish he was still around. I think he could have done more than he did. I hope so, at least. How do *you* feel?"

Her eyes welled with tears. "So dumb. I already cried about this. I'm so tired of crying."

I moved closer to her. She did not pull away. I tried to wipe the tears from her eyes, like a good guy would do in a story. My thumb jabbed into her eye.

"Ow," she said.

"Maybe not now, but soon we should probably talk about what we're going to-"

"I already went to the clinic." It came out fast, words tumbling from one to the next. She twisted her fingers together. It looked painful. "I talked to my mom, and she made a lot of sense. I'm sorry, I should have told you or invited you or something."

The roads and strip malls were suddenly so far away. Gravity had died and I was floating off the edge of the roof. Untethered and moving weightless to God knows where. It was terrifying and freeing. But no, I was sitting there on the roof with her and whatever bits of DNA were threatening to become a baby were gone. Poof. A disappearing act from the story that never was.

"Are you like, how do you feel?" I asked.

She shrugged. "It was weird, sort of. It didn't hurt very much, I was surprised. I don't... I don't feel any different and that feels... awful."

"You didn't need to tell me, it's... I get it." But I didn't get it. I didn't get anything. But I was glad that she was okay and had her future, so I said it again. "I get it."

"I do love you. But..."

"But you were always going to leave."

It took her a long time to answer. She looked out at all the nothingness and everything that lived in the little portal that we could view. A frame in a View-Master. Click, change. Click, change. Click, click, click give me more. I wondered what she saw out there. It had to be quite different from me.

"Yeah," she said. Then, "Where are you going to go?"

I didn't think it mattered if I stayed or went if I kept acting like an asshole. "I'm not sure yet," I said.

She moved next to me over the rough shingles of her roof. Closed the gap until our thighs were touching. She put her leg over mine. She asked, "Can I still do this?" and I nodded yes. She nestled the inseam of her Chuck into mine.

"Bread and butter."

"Bread and butter."

We looked through the View-Master, but it didn't change. Click. She asked me a question.

"What's something you love?"

ROCK CITY PLAYLIST

"A Losing Season" - Sorry About Dresden

The Complete Discocrappy - Charles Bronson

"Tuff Luff" - The Unicorns

"Love Rhymes with Hideous Car Wreck" - Blood Brothers

"Lover's Spit" - Broken Social Scene

"Tim, I Wish You Were Born a Girl" - of Montreal

"The Black Angel's Death Song" - Velvet Underground

"Lua" - Bright Eyes

Plague Soundscapes - The Locust

"Blue" - Whirlwind Heat

"Romantic Rights" - Death from Above 1979

"Agenda Suicide" - The Faint

"Art is Hard" - Cursive

"From the Back of the Film" - Thrush Hermit

"You and Me" - Archers of Loaf

"Tears Don't Matter Much (Live @ Cat's Cradle 9/24/2004)" - Lucero

"Oh My Sweet Carolina" - Ryan Adams

"Hurt" - Johnny Cash

“Watermark” - The Weakerthans

“Hoist That Rag” - Tom Waits

“Jesus, ETC.” - Wilco

The author in a field outside of Rocky Mount, NC, 2005.

Yes, that's a Mike's Hard Lemonade.

ACKNOWLEDGMENTS

I HAVE A LOT of people to thank, and I don't know when I'll get to do this again. Here goes.

JDO. You pushed me to make this book as good as it can be and then actually published the thing. Incredible.

Benjamin Whitmer for being an example when I was a younger man.

Todd Robinson. You published my first story, and it kept me going.

For the real ones, who were there: D. Montgomery, E. Hendrix, L. Fox, L. Covington, E. Riggins, H. Kanthak, A. Smiley, R. Murphy, and, of course, Big Dan the Man and the Peeknock clan. If I forgot you I'm sorry. Things are kinda hazy.

Cameron Strittmatter, Jesse Threatt, Dustin Gooch, Kevin Tadge, John Parson, Allie Stauffer. You guys read this and we're like, "It could be better." You were right.

Mr. Robert O'Brien, the best English teacher in Rocky Mount.

Wayne Crawford, as always.

My family. No. You already got the dedication, I think that's enough.

JoEllen, my person. I love you.

Made in the USA
Middletown, DE
29 March 2023